SEAL CAMP

Suzanne Brockmann

Suzanne Brockmann Books
www.SuzanneBrockmann.com

A Suzanne Brockmann Books Original
First publication: May 2018
Copyright © 2018 Suzanne Brockmann

Cover Design: Scott Fowler
Photographer: Rick Stockwell
Cover model: David Williams

www.SuzanneBrockmann.com
Email Newsletter: *News from Suz*: https://tinyletter.com/SuzanneBrockmann
www.BookBub.com/authors/suzanne-brockmann
www.Twitter.com/SuzBrockmann
www.Facebook.com/SuzanneBrockmannBooks

DEDICATION

For the resisters, the fighters, the bird-flipping bike riders, the #BlackLivesMatter marchers, the children who rise because we shamefully didn't, the Dreamers, the kneelers, the warrior celebrities who refuse to "shut up and sing," the comedians whose "jokes" help keep us sane even as they hold the line, the Nazi-punchers* and the peaceful sign-makers, the screamers and shouters, *the registered voters*, the stalwart believers in truth, hope, inclusive equality, and love.

Don't back down. Don't shut up. Don't give in. Keep fighting! Rise up! Your joyful noise and active participation are desperately needed. Fear, not hate, is the opposite of love. Courage, America. Don't let the fearful crush your love.

*Please be sure to punch all Nazis with love in your heart: Love for me, for my gay son and his beloved husband, and for all of my family, friends, and readers who are seen by those Nazis as "other," and for every Allied veteran of WWII, living and dead. Also, if punching with words alone doesn't work and you find you must use other means to protect the world from further Nazi harm, please take care not to hurt your hand. Thank you.

★   ★   ★

Special thanks to my kickass team of beta readers, and to all who supported the Kickstarter campaign for my latest rom-com movie, *Analysis Paralysis*.

CHAPTER ONE

Timeline: SEAL Camp *(TDD #12) is set* both *in the present day,* and *about a year and a half after the end of* Night Watch *(TDD #11). Embrace the time warp!*

Lieutenant Jim "Spaceman" Slade couldn't keep up as his SEAL Team ran across the barren desert.

True, his team for this training op was almost entirely tadpoles—relatively new additions to SEAL Team Ten—which meant they were significantly younger than he was.

In a world where you were the "old man" at twenty-eight, Jim's thirty-four years made him ancient. Especially for a big guy. And like most of the bigger SEALs in the Teams, Jim felt his advanced age most prominently in his rapidly decaying knees.

His men somehow knew he was hurting—his poker-face was perhaps a bit too tight—and they slowed down. For him.

A SEAL Team was only as fast as its slowest member.

And having a member as slow as Jim could get the entire team killed.

Not here, in this SoCal desert, a short helo ride from the Navy Base in Coronado, but out in the sandbox in A-stan and points unknown, for damn sure.

"Yo'kay, sir?" Petty Officer Rio Rosetti slowed to run beside Jim. He was one of those lean, compact, wiry guys. Provided he made chief, he'd probably still be a SEAL—and outrunning future tadpoles—well into his fifties.

But Jim couldn't hate the kid. He could only hate himself.

The other two tadpoles—Thomas King and David Williston, the newest member of Team Ten—joined Jim on his other side. King spoke up. "How can we help, sir?"

So Jim did something that he wouldn't've been able to do, had this been a Real World mission, and not just a training op.

He took himself out.

"New scenario," he told them, as he slowed to a stop. He wasn't out of breath—that wasn't the issue. He was aerobically fit. But his freaking knee—the left one, the "good" one—was on fire. "Your team leader—me—sustained a direct hit from a mortar round. There's nothing left; nothing to carry out; nothing to bring home." He looked at King who, as a lieutenant junior grade, was the highest ranking among them. "You're now in charge, Lieutenant. Complete the mission, and get your men safely to the extraction point."

Normally imperturbable, King's dark brown eyes widened just a little. "Aye, aye, sir, but before I leave you here, outside of the context of this training op, I must ask: do you need medical aid?"

"I can find my own freaking medical aid," Jim growled at the kid.

Now King didn't so much as blink. Clearly he'd made note of the fact that Jim had not said *no*. "With all due respect, LT—"

Jim cut him off. "I have my phone, I have flares, and I have a shit-ton of pain in my knee that's going to require another month or two of rest." At best. He'd just come off of an extended rest period, after having surgery on his "bad" knee, which was now his new "good" knee, which meant it was only throbbing in contrast to the stabbing fire lighting up the other. "Trust me, the few short minutes that I'll be alone after you leave and before the hospital corpsmen find me will be time well-spent, managing my goddamn frustration."

But King still hesitated.

Rio spoke up. "I'll hang back, sir," he addressed King, "just a bit, until the corpsmen make contact with the LT. Then I'll run to catch up."

The kid *was* faster than the rest of the team.

"I don't need a babysitter—" Jim started, but King cut him off.

"With all due respect, sir, *I'm* in command." He nodded to Rio—"Do it"—then turned to the rest of the men. "Let's go, move out."

And just like that, they were gone. Even Rio, who moved off with the team toward the horizon, where he'd hover to make sure… what? That Jim didn't get eaten by a giant sand lizard…?

He sighed as he used his phone to call for medical assistance, then sat down in the dirt to wait. The morning was hot and the sky was blue—and some kind of vulture circled closer to check him out.

"Screw you, asshole, I'm not dead yet."

He already knew what his options were. More surgery. He

didn't have to like it, he just had to do it. But he'd already had both knees done. He'd spent more time in the hospital and physical therapy in the past few years than he'd spent out on missions. And as much as he hated staying behind to heal and rest, he knew he'd hate it more if he went out on an op and couldn't keep up.

Which meant he'd have to face the idea of pulling himself permanently out of the Teams. Or—worse yet—getting pulled out.

Retirement.

Jesus.

The idea made his anger and frustration fade and left him feeling... what?

Tired. And empty.

As the helo with the medical team finally approached with a wash of noise from the blades, Jim stood and waved to Rio, who waved back and finally vanished, ready to run at his top speed for however many miles, probably without breaking much of a sweat.

The way Jim used to do when he first earned his Budweiser and joined Team Ten over a decade ago.

What was he, if couldn't be a Navy SEAL?

Lieutenant Jim Slade had absolutely no clue.

Ashley DeWitt quickly ducked behind the Dumpster that sat in the corner of her condo association's parking lot.

Dear, *sweet* God! The smell back here was horrific. Tomorrow morning was weekly garbage pickup day and the container was already overflowing. Add the heat of the southern California sun...

And yet here she crouched in full cowardly-hiding mode, despite the eyeball-melting stench.

She peeked around the corner and...

She quickly pulled back, because yes, that *was* Brad—not just some random man who looked vaguely Brad-like. Tall, lean, early thirties, with closely cropped light-brown hair and blue eyes, a lot of men looked like Brad. Particularly when he wore one of his expensive dark suits with a white shirt that showed off his gleamingly handsome, golf-tanned face.

After a year of silence, her crazy ex-boyfriend had begun emailing and calling again. *Can we meet? We really need to talk.*

She'd blocked and deleted, choosing to use silence as her answer. But now he'd shown up at her condo door—which was a little alarming because it had been years, plus a cross-country move, since she'd seen him last. During their tumultuous breakup, when Brad had gone into the worst of his *I know if I just keep showing up, you'll take me back* phase, she'd lived in Boston, in a student-level apartment in a relatively sketchy neighborhood, with her best friend Colleen.

But shortly after graduation from law school, Colleen had gotten married to the man of her dreams. She'd happily moved to Southern California, passed the bar, and gotten a job practicing family law in the San Diego suburb of San Felipe. It wasn't too long before she'd talked Ashley into moving out here, too, to work with her at the very same small law firm.

Colleen had wanted Ashley to move into the guest bedroom of the apartment she and her husband shared, mostly because she knew Ashley hated living alone. But they were newlyweds, so Ash had bought this condo with the money she'd inherited from her grandmother—her mother's mother—and tried her best to feel confident and safe.

Although, the truth was, Ashley couldn't remember a time since her incredibly protected and, yes, privileged childhood that she'd felt completely safe.

Which was why she spent a great deal of time exactly like this—quivering with fear as she hid from conflict.

Just this morning, over at the courthouse, she'd escaped into the ladies' room to avoid an altercation with Greg Ramsey, the always-angry husband of one of her clients. Ashley represented his soon-to-be-ex-wife Betsy in a messy divorce. And instead of standing her ground and coolly admonishing Mr. Ramsey over his inappropriateness, and reiterating that all communication between he and his wife needed to come through his lawyer, Ashley had chosen, instead, to hide from the man.

Truth was, she was a little afraid of him.

Real truth was, outside of the structured control of the courtroom, she was a little afraid of everyone and everything.

And okay, she wasn't *that* much of a wimp. She wasn't afraid of her younger brother Clark, and Clark's college roommate, Kenneth.

Yay?

As Ash peeked out from behind the Dumpster again, she saw Brad getting into a car parked in one of the slots set aside for visitors. Her heart sank as she saw that it was a black Lexus with darkly tinted windows and California plates. No way was that a rental car, which meant he was most likely living here again, in California, where he'd gone to college, and a mix of fear and anger made her throat tighten.

She'd slept better when he'd lived on the other side of the country, in New York. Not because she thought he'd hurt her. He wasn't violent, he wasn't even close to a psycho stalker. At least she didn't *think* he was.

But she was afraid that he was right. And that if he pressured her hard enough, she'd do something really stupid and weak, like finally give in, forgive his lies, and take him back.

As Ashley watched, Brad started his car's engine, the red taillights flashing on. But he didn't pull out, and he didn't pull out, and as she realized that he wasn't leaving, her heart dropped ever farther. He was just going to sit in his car with the air conditioner on, waiting for her to come home.

And, God help her, she was too much of a coward to face him.

Her phone rang, and she immediately silenced it, glancing at the screen and... The universe was presenting her with an awesome *Exhibit A*. Her father was calling again, to give her his daily pitch on why she should move back to New York and join his prestigious law firm. She didn't need to take the call—she'd heard his words often enough. *What are you doing out there, working for lower wages than you'd get even as a public defender? Come home to Scarsdale, where you belong. You've proven your point. You win—I'll fast-track you to partner. You'll have a corner office, and in just a few years, your name'll be beneath mine on the door...*

But really, she didn't *want* to take the call. Instead, she'd hide from her ongoing battle with her father by letting him go to voicemail. She'd respond later, via email. *Sorry, too busy with work to talk. Hope you're well, hugs to Cynthia...*

Instead, she checked her email as she hid back behind the Dumpster, breathing through her mouth. She responded to a message from her boss, Jessica Rae Cofer. The local women's shelter had approached their tiny firm with another pro bono request. Another battered woman, like Betsy Ramsey, attempting to legalize her separation from a monster through divorce. Did Ashley have time to add another non-paying client to her already busy schedule?

Of course, she did. Always. Ash quickly fired back her response.

There was an email about a scheduling issue from opposing counsel on one of her paying cases, so she checked her calendar and responded to that email, too.

It was while she was answering another email from her little brother Clark—*No, if he adopted a shelter dog, she would* not *be able to dog-sit for him. Yes, she loved dogs and yes, she was a pushover, but her condo association had a strict no-pets rule, sorry*—that she realized that she was simply accepting her fate.

She'd reached the point where she'd prefer to spend god-knows-how-long hiding from her life behind a stank-fest of a Dumpster rather than risking getting upset—or facing someone else's potential upset, anger, or disappointment.

Something had to change.

She had to change.

On impulse, she texted Colleen. *Is that trained-by-a-Navy-SEAL class thing you were telling me about still open?*

Colleen's husband was a man-mountain of a Navy SEAL chief named Bobby Taylor, and he'd told Colleen—who'd told Ash—about a week-long class at a place called SEAL World, run by a former SEAL chief named Duncan Something. Or maybe it was Something Duncan...? Anyway, his class combined Outward-Bound type activities with exercises designed to boost self-confidence. Participants—mostly corporate types—apparently gained self-respect and self-esteem through the physical challenges.

Colleen didn't text back—she called. "I'm looking it up right now," she said, without any greeting. She'd been wanting Ashley to take this course ever since she'd first found out about it, years ago. "And yes, Dunk's website says—whoa! He's had a cancellation. He's usually completely sold out, but there're still a few slots open for a class that starts... oh, this Saturday."

"Saturday?" Ash echoed. It was already Thursday. "Crap, that's too soon."

"No, it's not," Colleen said. "It's actually perfect. It gives us just enough time to get together, so you can fill me in on your cases—so I can handle anything that comes up while you're away." She raised her voice, calling to their boss, who always worked with her office door open. "Jess, you okay with Ashley taking off for a week, to take that Navy SEAL class thing I was telling you about? I'll cover for her."

Ashley could hear Jess calling back, "Yes, absolutely!"

"I'll come over tonight," Colleen told Ashley. "You'll have time tomorrow to shop for any gear that you might need—but not enough time to second guess yourself and get scared."

"Yeah, thanks, I'm already terrified," Ashley said. "I don't know, Col. I had this flash of *Maybe I need to do something*, but now…"

"Why are you whispering?" Colleen asked.

"Um…"

"Are you hiding in some bathroom again?" Her friend's voice was not unkind. "Look around you. Take a moment and take a deep breath. Is this really where you want to be? I believe, completely, that you are *so* much stronger than you think. And I think this class is exactly what you need so that you can start believing that, too."

Ashley looked around, but didn't dare take a deep breath. Colleen was right. She had to do this. And she was ready. Or at least as ready as she'd ever be. "Can you do me a huge favor?" she asked her friend. "And sign me up…? Right now…? On the website…? Use your credit card—I'll pay you back."

"We're past the date where you can cancel and get a refund," Colleen warned her.

"I know," Ash said. She'd surfed the SEAL World website many times, wishing she were brave enough to take the plunge. "Do it. Now. Quickly, please, before I chicken out!"

Jim sat in his truck.

He knew he had to turn the key, start the engine, drive out of the Navy base. He had to pick up something for dinner at the grocery store. He had to go home, ice his knees, cook his dinner, ice his knees, eat, and again ice his knees. Twenty minutes at a time.

He had to rest.

That was the doctor's order—and it was a literal order because the doc was a captain, and outranked Jim. *Get a coupla weeks of rest while the medical team reviews these latest MRIs and scans. At that point, we'll take another look, and talk about your options.*

When the captain said that, he'd seen Jim's face, and had both sighed and chuckled. Based in Coronado, the man saw a lot of injured SEALs, and he knew that, to them, *rest* was the nastiest of all of the four-letter words.

It had been four years since Jim had taken any leave that wasn't connected to rehabbing his injured knees—it was all right there in his record.

So as the doc signed the necessary papers, he'd clarified. *Take a real vacation. No running, no basketball, no jumping out of airplanes. Exercise in moderation, preferably in a swimming pool, with a daiquiri in your hand. Walking is okay—in moderation—to get from your room to the hotel lounge. Feet up when you can, and plenty of ice. Make use of the time off, Lieutenant. Visit family or friends.*

In other words, get the hell not just out of his office and off the base, but out of California, too.

Jim knew not to push and ask exactly what *options* the doc thought the medical team might come up with. Best case would be more surgery, while the nightmare scenario would be horrific. Desk job A or desk job B. Oh, hey, maybe he could teach. Be a BUD/S classroom instructor. *That* would be fun...

A tap on his window made him jump. Great, he was already losing his edge.

But it was Thomas King, the young lieutenant who'd taken command during the training op. His buddies Dave and Rio were with him, but they were standing back a bit.

"We're heading over to the bar, sir," King said as Jim put his window down. "You up for a burger and a beer?" He smiled. He didn't smile often, but when he did, it transformed his usually stern visage and made him look more like the twenty-something kid that he was. "Rio's buying."

As one of the many men of color in the SEAL Teams—and King's skin tone was a very dark brown, which meant that to certain parts of white-bread America he was the quintessential image of a "big, scary" black man—Thomas King had earned his right to become both a SEAL and an officer. And yet he *still* got mistaken for an enlisted man, particularly when he was dressed in BDUs, thanks to ingrained assumptions and willful ignorance. On top of *that* insulting goatfuckery, Lieutenant King could return Stateside from a dangerous mission and get his ass shot and killed simply from walking down the street, or standing in his backyard, or shopping in a department store.

So maybe it made sense that Thomas King was the only man who had the big enough balls to invite him to go out with them, particularly since Jim had been sitting here glowering at the world.

Still, he knew that King and the other tadpoles didn't *really* want his company. And he didn't want theirs. He was at the end of his career, and they were right at the beginning—with all that hope and promise and excitement in front of them. "Thanks, but no," Jim said. "I'm heading home."

King turned away, but then turned back. "You know Senior Chief Duncan, right, sir? Randy Duncan...? Dunk? Left the Teams about two years ago?"

Of course Jim knew Dunk. Everyone knew Dunk—a salty old senior chief, who'd been with Team Two since forever. He was one of those lean, wiry guys who ran marathons for fun. Dunk had lost a leg in Afghanistan while literally saving a busload of nuns and orphans, and had since learned to walk and run with a prosthetic. He'd even had the chance to stay with the Teams, but chose instead to leave. Last Jim had heard, Dunk had hiked out to Machu Picchu with a long-time civilian friend.

"Message received, Lieutenant," Jim said. Unlike Dunk, he still had both legs, both firmly attached. Time to stop feeling sorry for himself.

But King looked surprised and then dismayed. "Oh, no, sir," he quickly said. "I haven't gotten to the message, which is that Dunk started a boot camp for, well, corporate types who want a challenge."

"Yeah, I'd heard he was doing that," Jim said.

"Every session's filled," King told him, "Even if someone drops out, there's always someone else ready to take their spot. He's got a week-long class that starts on Saturday, and one of his regular instructors—Deak Lundlee, you know, Crocodile Lundlee...?"

"I'm well acquainted with Croc," Jim said.

"Well, Croc's gotta drop out because Sheila, his wife, got the flu and... Anyway, Dunk called me, to see if maybe I could talk Dave or maybe even Mike Lee into coming with Rio and me, to replace Croc, but..." He shook his head. "Mike's out of the country and Dave can't break free. But then I thought of you."

"Train a group of SEAL wannabes," Jim said dryly. "Oh, joy."

"The money's insane," King told him bluntly. "And it's not awful. Like I said, it's only a week and... well, it's not exactly fun.

But it's fun-ish."

Jim looked at him. "Quite the ringing endorsement."

"Dunk's great," King said with a shrug. "And Lieutenant O'Donlon's an instructor this session, too. Syd, his wife, is going on some kind of writing retreat, so…"

Luke O'Donlon—known by his nickname *Lucky*—tended to be a walking party.

"Why on earth do you spend your downtime teaching at Dunk's camp?" Jim had to ask.

King glanced over his shoulder to where Rio and Dave were both checking their phones for email and texts. He lowered his voice. "To be honest, sir, I've been avoiding this… well, girl. She's way too young, so… it helps if I make myself scarce whenever I can."

That made sense.

"Dunk's camp is just outside of Sarasota, in Florida. West Coast—Gulf of Mexico. Can't beat the location. This time of year, the weather's perfect."

This time of year, the weather was pretty damn perfect in San Diego, too.

"I'm just saying that you could get rest *and* make some cash," King continued. "Dunk's still got the scooters he used when he first got out of the hospital, and he still gets around in a golf cart—I know he's got more than one. Plus, he's a great guy and you'd be helping him out. He told me he's gonna have to cancel the session if he can't replace Crocodile. So *I'm* begging you, too—I have the next few weeks free, and I *cannot* stay here in town."

Jim sighed. "My grumpy ass presence is gonna cancel out O'Donlon's blinding golden glee. You know that right?"

King smiled. "Believe me, I'm plenty good with fun-*ish*. I need distance—and the cash isn't gonna hurt. Is it okay with you if I text Dunk with your number?"

"He's already got it," Jim said. He knew Dunk well. "But yeah. Have him call me."

"Thank you, sir," King said as he backed away, fast. "You won't regret this."

"I already do," Jim grumbled, but Thomas King and his buddies were already gone.

CHAPTER TWO

Ashley's brother Clark was standing near the baggage claim at the Sarasota airport.

No, strike that. It was Ashley's brother Clark *and* his friend Kenneth. They were both in Sarasota.

Today, Clark's hair was Spike-from-*Buffy-the-Vampire-Slayer* white. Complete with dark roots. Since his blue-hair phase, he'd gone purple, then green—that didn't last because it completely didn't work with his pale skin tone and gray eyes—and even *Little Orphan Annie* red. Without the curls, thank goodness.

And despite Clark's dyed-haired rebellion against their too-strict, too-conservative father, he was here. To... what? Ashley wasn't sure.

"If you've come to talk me out of this," she started as she approached him.

But Clark's surprise at seeing her was genuine. Surprise that turned to immediate dismay. "Ah, fuh—"

She stopped him. "Let me guess. Dad signed you and Kenneth up for a cool week-long program at a camp just south of Sarasota, run by a former Navy SEAL. Without telling you that his real intention was for you to babysit me while I took the same course. God, I knew I shouldn't've mentioned it to him..." She looked at Kenneth. "Hey, Kenneth."

"Nice to see you, Ashley." Kenneth, tall and pale and skinny, with reddish hair and brown eyes hidden behind the slightly smudged lenses of stylishly black-framed glasses, hailed from the UK and was terminally polite.

"No, it's not," Ash said. "Neither you, nor Clark, nor I think that this is even remotely nice."

"Yes, of course that's true," Kenneth agreed. "But... You *are* looking... lovely."

"She looks like crap," her brother countered. "You sleeping?"

"Not much, not lately," Ashley informed him crisply. "I don't suppose I can talk you into just... not showing up? For the camp thing? Maybe go somewhere else for spring break…?"

But she could see in Clark's eyes that he actually wanted to do it. It made sense. They both needed help in the backbone-growing department.

"Never mind. It's okay," she continued. "Just promise you won't actually report back to Dad."

"Look at it this way," Kenneth spoke up, attempting to bright-side things. "In order to keep tabs on you, he might've hired some total stranger, and you would never have known…" His voice trailed off as he realized that Ashley and Clark's father had done exactly that in the past. Her ex, Brad, had been an employee of their father's—promised a partnership in the firm if he could convince Ashley to marry him.

"Sorry," Kenneth muttered, because, yes, that was *still* humiliating on every level.

"This was supposed to be my birthday present," Clark told Ashley. "I mean, I *thought* it was. I mean, I know I shouldn't've, because… *Dad*, right? Nothing comes for free."

"You know what?" Ashley interrupted him, looking from Clark to Kenneth and back. "This is going to be fun. We are going to have fun. Fuck Dad."

"Dude!" Clark laughed his surprise. Ashley did *not* drop F-bombs often.

"You'll report back to him," Ash continued as the luggage carousel lurched to life, "and by *you*, I mean, *I'll* borrow your phone, and text him for you. I can't wait until he finds out about my torrid affair with Kenneth."

Clark laughed as Kenneth choked. "What?"

"I know you're young," Ashley said, "but it was meant to be." As Kenneth continued to cough, she patted him on the back as she laughed. "Relax, I'm just kidding, you're practically my brother. Although you have to admit, Dad would be appalled."

The hot blonde traveling with her own private two-man boy band laughed, and again caught Jim's eye.

She was pretty, if you were into angels or fairy princesses—with her blond hair cut strikingly short, her pale blue eyes, and her porcelain doll complexion. She was dressed down in jeans and a blue T-shirt, running shoes on her feet—but her clothes looked new and slightly uncomfortable.

As Jim watched, her teenaged companions wrestled a giant purple suitcase off of Sarasota Airport's baggage claim conveyor belt, along with a smaller red-plaid one. The fairy princess already had a wheeled carry-on bag, so the two boys manhandled her larger ones as she pointed toward the restrooms and they all moved off in that direction.

It was then that Dunk came in from the sliding doors that led to the parking lot. The former SEAL chief was looking healthy and relaxed—his salt-and-pepper hair was longer than he'd ever worn it in the Teams, curling around his ears. His face was tanned and he kept his wraparound shades on. He wore a SEAL Team Two T-shirt over cargo shorts—one leg sinewy with a flip-flop on his foot, the other carbon fiber with a running blade at the end.

He spotted Jim and grinned as he shouted across the terminal. "Yo, asshole, how ya doing?"

Jim laughed as he went to shake the man's hand. "Asshole? That's nice, considering I'm here to save you."

"I know, and thank you." Dunk pulled him in for a hug disguised as a chest bump. "I'm just celebrating my freedom as a civilian. I've said *sir* enough for a lifetime, so I'm playing with all possible alternatives."

Jim laughed again. "You look good."

"You, my friend, look like shit on a stick. Knees hurting bad, huh?"

"I'll live."

Dunk got serious. "That doesn't cut it, man. You can't just live with the hand you're dealt, you gotta live *well*." But then he grinned again. "You know, leaving the Teams doesn't have to mean that your best days are over. That's just a myth."

Jim felt his hackles rise. "Yeah, well, I'm not ready to leave the Teams yet. This is just a break while the doctors figure out which operation will fix my shit for good."

Dunk gave him a measured look. "We all leave, eventually. One way or another. I'm just saying it doesn't have to suck. I finally did some of that traveling I'd always wanted to do. Paris, Berlin, London—you know, with time to look around and visit an art museum or two. Iceland rocked. Fjords of Norway—via cruise ship while I was still in the chair, and then again, camping. Saw the midnight sun and then the Northern Lights. Oh, and *fuhhhking* Easter Island! *That* was crazy."

Jim nodded. "And Machu Picchu. I saw the pics you posted on the Team message board."

"Like I said, I'm living well. I know you can't quite let yourself believe it, but it's been pretty great. And the camp's been fun. And lucrative. Everyone and their little brother wants to pretend to be a SEAL. Glad young Thomas talked you into joining our merry band."

"Yeah," Jim said. "I'm not sure *I'm* glad yet. I'll let you know. Oh, message from O'Donlon. He's on the same flight as Thomas and Rio—into Tampa, arriving tonight. He's going to rent a car, so no need to pick them up."

"Thanks," Dunk said. "That's good to know. I'm going to text him, see if he can't also shuttle a pair of campers who are prolly coming in on that same flight. And speaking of campers, I'm picking up the first arrivals right now. Three of 'em…"

Jim realized that Dunk had been holding a clipboard beneath one arm. It had a sign taped on the back saying *SEAL World*. Dunk now held it up in front of him, and Jim stepped back a bit so as not to block it.

It would be interesting to see the kind of guys who would sign up for this type of boot camp session and…

Holy shit, the princess and her boy band had come out of the bathrooms, pointed straight at Dunk, and were now heading directly toward them.

Jim turned and looked behind them, but no, there was no car rental counter back there—just the terminal wall. They were definitely heading for Dunk and his sign.

The princess faltered slightly as she met Jim's disbelieving eyes. Her own were wide and such a light shade of blue that they were practically crystal gray. She was almost ridiculously, strikingly beautiful—but if she'd appeared in a line-up of potential SEAL World campers, she'd be the dead-last person Jim would pick as someone willing to spend money on anything other than a trip to the mall. With the boy-band coming in *just* above her.

"Uh-oh," Dunk muttered.

"So… this is not typical?" Jim muttered back, just to confirm.

"Not even close," Dunk muttered. "We're inclusive, of course, and we occasionally get women, which is great, but I do like to have advance planning, because, well... Some campers aren't as open to letting girls into their boys-only playtime. In fact, I've been thinking about offering a women-only class, but... We're picking up what I *thought* were brothers. Clark and A. DeWitt. And someone else named... Ken Price."

"Maybe the kids are Clark and A," Jim offered, "and she's just the incredibly hot nanny...?"

Oops, he'd said that a little too loud—she was close enough to have heard him, and her mouth tightened as her cheeks flushed. But she aimed a smile at Dunk as she asked, "Are you Senior Chief Duncan? I'm Ashley. DeWitt. The *lawyer* from California....?"

The A stood for Ashley, and she was a lawyer, not a nanny. Jim knew that last piece of info was for him, even though she didn't deign to look at him again.

In fact, she barely glanced in his direction, even after she'd introduced her brother Clark—the Spike-the-vampire wannabe—and his friend Kenneth-not-Ken-with-the-Colin-Firth-accent. Even when Dunk intro'd Jim as one of his new camp instructors, she only gave him the vaguest of polite smiles.

As they walked out into the brilliance of the day, heading to the parking lot, Ashley chatted easily with Dunk. It wasn't until they got to the SEAL World van that Jim caught up and realized they were talking about the technology behind Dunk's prosthetic, which was interesting. Most people either stared or ignored—he would've taken Ashley for a full-on ignorer.

Or maybe *Jim* was the one that she was going to ignore for the entire week.

A few short miles outside of Sarasota, the suburbs rapidly vanished, giving way to orange groves and fields of cattle.

And although the camp was well off the main road, the compound was far less rustic than Ashley had feared it would be. It was located at the site of an old RV park, and the participants were housed in a motley collection of ancient but well-kept trailers in all shapes and sizes. Some were streamlined and white, some were bubble-shaped and shiny silver, some were square and brightly colored. All were hooked up to water and electricity, but instead of being parked close together in tight rows, they were scattered throughout the sandy-soiled, pine-and-palm-treed campground, nestled in their own private patches of shade.

It was actually quite charming.

As was Dunk. During the drive, Ashley'd had a chance to tell him that she was close friends with Colleen and Bobby Taylor—and he knew Chief Taylor well. As did Lieutenant Jim Slade—the significantly *less* charming giant SEAL instructor who'd called her a *hot nanny*.

"I've got to reorganize the barracks assignments before I hand out keys," Dunk announced after he'd parked the van in front of the big central building that bore the sign *Mess Hall*. He grinned at Ashley as he led them inside. "I'd originally given you the double, put you in with your brother, but—"

"Oh, God, no, please and thank you," Ash said. The spacious room was filled with long picnic-styled tables with attached benches. An open counter looked into a large kitchen.

Dunk laughed. "Yeah, that's what I thought."

"Kenneth, are you okay sharing with Clark?" Ash asked.

"Of course."

"You can just switch me and Kenneth," she told Dunk.

"Yeah, no," Dunk said. "I mean, essentially yes, that *is* what I'll do. I just need to check where I put Ken and… My office is right here—" he pointed to a door. "Give me ten to do that administrative work. In the meantime, feel free to wander. Gedunk's over there—" he pointed toward a small alcove off the mess hall that bore a sign *Honor Gedunk* "—lounge is in the back." And with that he was gone.

"What's a *Gedunk*?" Ashley asked Clark as she went to look. Was it some sort of play on the man's nickname?

The walls of the alcove were lined with tables that were filled with SEAL World hats and T-shirts and sweatshirts, as well as snacks and supplies from a drug store. Cold meds and Tylenol and shampoo and Q-tips.

"*Gedunk* is Navy slang for the place on a ship where sailors can buy snacks and sundries."

She looked up to see the annoying Lieutenant Slade leaning against the alcove's frame. He'd been limping—just a little—as they'd walked to the parking lot of the airport.

"I always liked that word: *sundries*," he added with a smile that softened his harshly craggy features. With his sparkling blue eyes and dark, wavy hair she might've even found him handsome, had he not already proven himself to be a first-class idiot.

He pointed to an iPad that was permanently attached to one of the tables with something that looked like a bicycle lock. "If there's something you need, you scan the barcode. I bet five dollars Dunk's gonna give everyone their own PIN."

"That makes sense," she said politely, smiling slightly in his general direction as she went past him, back into the mess hall.

"Whoa, Kenneth, check this out!" Clark exclaimed as he and his friend disappeared through the door labeled *Lounge*.

She followed them in—it was a fairly large room that had clearly once been a kid's arcade—filled with pool and foosball tables, pinball machines, and even old-school, ancient video games.

"Oh, my God, this is an original Space Invaders!" Kenneth howled, forgetting to be British in his delight.

"PacMan's set for five games for a quarter!" Clark, too, was over the moon.

"Space Invaders is, too!"

Ashley was more interested in the bamboo bar that stretched across a full wall. This was clearly an evening hangout area where the campers could socialize. There were several craft beers on tap, plus a large wine fridge. Like the Gedunk, it was serve yourself, although a sign proclaimed a reasonable two drink limit.

Another sign said *We reserve the right to close this bar at any time for any reason.*

That, too, seemed fair.

The boys had found a change machine, but couldn't get it to work. "There's nowhere to insert anything." Kenneth was puzzled. "Not dollar bills or credit cards. It just keeps asking for my PIN."

"I'm pretty sure the whole camp's designed so you don't have to carry any cash or cards." The giant SEAL had followed her again. "Or keys. The trailers are locked with keypads."

"Do you have any quarters?" Clark asked Ashley.

"I don't," she said. She'd cleaned out her bag before this trip, and she'd used her credit card for the coffee she'd bought in the airport.

"I got a few." Lieutenant Slade had two quarters in the palm of his giant hand.

"Oh," she said. "No, that's okay," even as Clark exclaimed "Yes! Thank you!" as he grabbed them and ran.

"He's twenty, going on twelve," she told the man. "I'll make sure he pays you back."

"I'm not worried," he said with another charismatic smile. "So how long have you known Colleen Taylor?"

"Since college," she said politely. "We were roommates."

"Lucky you," he said. "She's amazing. I'm one of the many in Team Ten who had a crush on her. Before she married Bobby, I tried to get her brother—Wes—to set us up."

"She is really great." That was one thing—and possibly the only thing—they'd ever agree upon. Ashley gave the lieutenant a distant smile that she hoped he'd read as completely disinterested as she headed for the side door.

Just as she'd suspected, it led to an outside patio where there was a large, gorgeous swimming pool with an attached hot-tub. Lounge chairs and umbrellas were positioned around it, their fabric in various shades of blue. It looked more like a resort than a boot camp.

Outside of the pool's fence was what looked like a playground, with a colorful rock-climbing wall, and a variety of other obstacles and challenges.

"That's a smaller, less dangerous version of the BUD/S O-course." Lieutenant Slade had followed her, again. He misread her frustration as confusion and gave her another of those smiles. "BUD/S stands for Basic Underwater Demolition-slash-SEAL. It's the training we all go through to become SEALs. At first it's not so much about the underwater demolition—it's more about PT—physical training. On base, there's a really punishing obstacle course that we have to complete in shorter and shorter amounts of time, both individually, and in teams. Even scaled down like this, it can really help with team-building."

"Team building?" she said with dismay. God, he was going to think she was an idiot, only able to parrot his own words back at him. Except, really, why should she care what this man thought about her. *Hot nanny*... True, she'd have to interact with him for the next week, but after that, she'd never see him again. "I didn't realize that we were going to be working together with the other campers."

"Yeah," he said, amusement in his eyes. "It's SEAL *Team*. Rambo's a myth—or at least he wasn't SpecOps, Navy. If you ever read a book where the SEAL character is described as a *loner*, you throw that book against the wall. Hard."

"These days I mostly read on my iPad," she told him.

He laughed. "Okay, then, hit delete, or, what...? Archive, right?"

She gave him another unfocused smile as she turned back to the door, but this time he blocked her.

"Look," he continued. "Before you go in, or before Thing 1 and Thing 2 come crashing out here to shriek about the awesome awesomeness of the pool, I'd... well, I'd really like to apologize."

Ashley finally looked up and met his eyes squarely for the first time since she'd seen him in the airport. They were unbelievably blue, and for once his relentless amusement was tempered—he was dead serious.

"I know you overheard my incredibly inappropriate *hot nanny* comment and I am so sorry—not that you overheard, but that I said it," he told her. "I was making a joke—trying to and failing doubly since it wasn't even funny. I not only disrespected you, but I'm guilty of judging and valuing you based on your appearance instead of your whole self. And that sucks. I should know better because people often look at me and peg me as a knuckle-dragging, mouth-breathing asshole. And that's only true a fraction of the time."

She was so surprised—she was standing there with her own mouth slightly open. So she closed it. Cleared her throat.

But the lieutenant didn't seem to expect her to say anything, whether it was to accept his apology or not. He opened the door to the lounge for her. "Come on. Dunk's probably ready for us. I'll help you get your suitcases to your bunk."

Ashley found her voice as he followed her back inside. "That's okay. I don't need help. I followed the instructions on the website—it said to pack light, in a single suitcase, to leave valuables at home, and be ready to carry our own bag over uneven terrain."

"Wait," he said, "that giant purple bag's not yours?"

She stopped to look at him. "And why would you assume that it is?"

Because women stereotypically over-pack? She knew he was thinking along those lines and realized he'd put his foot in it, again, but instead he said, "The, uh, color...?"

"Have you met Clark?" she said, starting for the mess hall. "When he got that bag, a few months ago, it matched his hair."

He laughed. "Of course it did. Well, I apologize, yet again."

"I'm also a really good driver," Ashley told him, "and I happen to be great at science and math. And everyone's gonna hate having me on their team. Am I the only woman here this session? I am, right? I honestly don't know how I missed that detail about team-building on the website..."

"You can be on my team," Lieutenant Slade said. "You, me, Clark, and Kenneth."

"Kinda like sitting at the kiddie table," Ash murmured. She sighed. "I was actually hoping to learn something, but okay. At least I won't ruin anyone else's SEAL World experience."

CHAPTER THREE

"Hot tip. Slower runners stay to the left of the trail," the camper nicknamed Bull mansplained to Ashley. "That way, you won't get in the way of those of us who're faster."

Big and beefy and dressed in camo gear that made them look ridiculous, he and his friend Todd had been to SEAL World before, and were filled with all kinds of condescending information.

Ashley's first night had been uneventful, but mostly because she'd retreated to her RV. After unpacking her gear, she'd taken her dinner back to her trailer—the mess was serving pre-made sandwiches since campers would be arriving all through the evening hours—and gone to bed early. She was hoping to get her body attuned to the eastern time zone as quickly as possible.

Now, as the campers gathered in the sandy clearing outside of the mess hall in the dawn light, Bull had approached her to ask if she was one of the instructor's girlfriends, hired on for the session as kitchen help.

She was dressed exactly as he was—in running shorts and sneakers, since they'd been told the session would kick off with a group run.

When she'd told him, "No," and gone back to stretching, he'd then asked, "What, so you're a local hire, then?"

She'd finally told him what should've been obvious, "I'm here as a camper. Just like you."

Bull had laughed at that—first in astonishment, and then in horror. "Please God don't let her be on our team," he said to his buddy Todd, but loudly enough for Ash to hear him. "Most of us are here to get away from babysitting lesser-thans. Jesus. Just what we need. A girl on the team. Although, I've always said that the only thing this place is lacking is a few strategically placed camp followers, heh-heh, if you know what I mean. How about it, Ashley? You up for making some Benjamins on the side, in a little late night one-on-one?"

As the two men laughed, Ashley didn't respond—she just drifted away. Although, when she looked up, the big SEAL instructor named Lieutenant Slade was watching her closely. He was standing there, planted like a tree, legs slightly spread, big arms folded across his broad chest. He had on cargo shorts today—and had support braces on both knees.

"Listen up, people!" Dunk sped around the camp in an electric vehicle that was a cross between a golf cart and a dune buggy—the tires were designed to handle the soft sand—and he now stood on the driver's seat, holding onto the roll bar to address the campers.

There were twenty-five of them gathered there—and Ash was indeed the only woman.

What drugs had she been on, when she'd thought coming here would be a good idea...?

"This run is not a contest or a race," Dunk said.

"This is totally both a contest and a race." Ash turned to see that Bull had followed her. Great.

"Your task today is to get a baseline," Dunk continued. "With this run, and with all of the activities throughout the day."

"It's all a contest," Bull also continued. "Up at the range, in the pool, and running the O-course, too—although I'll bet you're great at the O. Uhhh, ohhh, uhnnn!" He made orgasm sounds. "Except, oops, it's not that kind of O. Too bad, huh? I'm pretty freaking good at *that* kind of O, myself. Happy to show you, anytime you want..."

God. Ashley moved away from him.

"We're also looking to create teams," Dunk continued. "We will be grouping you with six other men—" he caught himself "—other *people* who have different skills set than you. So you may not complete this run with the fastest time. That's okay. You might instead excel in the obstacle course, or up at the shooting range."

Shooting range. Ashley was dismayed. That's what Bull had meant by *range.* She was not at all interested in learning how to fire a gun.

"If you have not yet disclosed any recent injuries or physical limitations please do so now," Dunk continued as Ashley once more moved away from Bull. She tried to focus on listening as the former senior chief ran through the fine-print of the agreement that everyone should've already read, and then introduced them to Lieutenant Thomas King, the camp's almost impossibly young hospital corpsman—which was apparently Navy-Speak for *medic.*

Dunk then introduced the other SEAL instructors. In addition to

Lieutenants King and Slade, there was a Lieutenant O'Donlon and a Petty Officer Rosetti. O'Donlon was gleaming and golden, while Rosetti was possibly even younger than Lieutenant King—or maybe that was just an illusion because he was compact and wiry compared to the taller men.

And yet Jim Slade towered over them all....

"I want to stress the fact that our hospital corpsman, Lieutenant King, will be floating free," Dunk was still saying, "and—I repeat—his authority will override your instructor's *and* your team leader's."

"Team leaders...?" Wait, weren't the instructors the team leaders, but crap, Ashley had actually spoken aloud, and Bull had heard her.

"Each team elects a leader from the campers," he told her. "You should totally volunteer to do it. It's fun."

Now, why did she get the sense that it would be anything *but*...? Ashley moved away from him again as Dunk ran through the last of the rules—what would happen if a camper decided to drop out.

"If, at any time, you suddenly doubt your ability to make it through the program," he told them, "we urge you to talk to an instructor about modifications that can and will be made to the various exercises. Trust me, we can make it work—said the man with one leg." He laughed. "I'm hopeful this class will indeed trust me, but history says that two of you will be gone by tonight; another two by tomorrow, and five more by Monday. Don't let it be you."

"Or do." Bull was back. He was standing so close, his breath moved the tendrils of hair on Ashley's neck. "*Do* let it be you."

Ashley didn't move. She just closed her eyes and waited for Dunk to signal the start of the run.

All during Dunk's speech, Jim had watched the big idiot with the shaved head and the camo-print T-shirt pursue the woman. She'd kept moving away from him, yet he'd followed and followed again. From the smirk on the man's fugly face, and from the color in Ashley's cheeks, Jim knew that he was being a total tool.

Dunk had warned Jim about the guy. His nickname was Bull, and he and his friend Todd had attended SEAL World twice before. On a scale of zero to douche, he was a double-douche.

Each time he'd followed Ashley and said something no-doubt

inappropriate or rude, Jim had expected her to turn around and lay into the guy.

But she didn't. And she didn't. And she didn't again.

The whistle blew, and the woman took off—faster than almost everyone else.

She had runner's legs—long and muscular. She looked and acted like a powder puff pushover, but in fact, she was strong.

Jim powered up his electric dirt bike and surged ahead to catch up with her. "Hey, Ashley," he called, and she turned to look at him, her blue eyes shaded beneath her Red Sox cap. "Remember to pace yourself. Gonna be a long day."

She nodded—so serious—and kept running.

Jim saw right away that Ashley hated her time at the shooting range. She tried to duck out of it, using her negotiating skills as an attorney to attempt to "opt out," but Jim hardened his heart and didn't let her do it.

So as he'd watched, she'd closed her eyes and she'd fired her weapon. She did about as well as could be expected—considering that she'd closed her eyes as she'd fired her weapon.

The O-course was a fiasco for her, too. She had little-to-no upper body strength, and most of the obstacles required strong arms and shoulders. But her brother Clark and his friend Kenneth had stepped up—helping her along.

They were the only ones out of the other twenty-five campers who hadn't just blown past Ashley.

She'd killed it, however, on the pop calc quiz that the campers had been hit with immediately after lunch. She wasn't lying when she said she had math skills.

By 1600, they were done. The campers had free time to clean up before dinner as Jim headed into Dunk's office to help create the teams.

Thomas King and Lucky O'Donlon were already in there. Lucky was sprawled on the big leather sofa, while Thomas sat in a hard-backed chair. He rose as Jim came in, clearly offering him the seat.

"Jeez, King, I'm not your eighty-year-old grandpa," Jim said, but then realized that, yeah, maybe he was, since the only other places to sit were that too-soft sofa—with his knees at their current level of agony, he'd need a forklift to pull him out of there—or the chair on castors behind Dunk's desk. And no way was he taking Dunk's seat.

"Of course not, sir," Thomas said smoothly. "I was saving it for you, due to your *temporary* issues. See, with these arm rests…?"

Jim would be able to push himself back to his feet without embarrassing himself. "Thanks, man," he murmured as he took Thomas's seat.

"De nada, sir," Thomas murmured back. "I got you. Your being here is saving my ass."

From whoever that girl was, who'd obviously taken one look at the young SEAL with his handsome face, his BUD/S-hardened muscles, his ramrod straight posture, and his brilliant leader's mind combined with the empathic compassion of a hospital corpsman… Whoever she was, the girl was no fool.

But then Rio Rosetti came in, with Dunk right behind him. As always, Rio was talking up a storm.

"He's an asshole, is what he is, Senior," he was earnestly telling Dunk. "And if he ends up on *my* team, I cannot guarantee he'll survive the session."

"Let me guess," Thomas said dryly. "We're talking about Bull Edison."

"We are," Dunk admitted.

Even Lucky made a face. "I say we rotate him and his idiot friend, what's his name, Tom?"

"Todd," Jim said in unison with Thomas and Rio.

"That's not a bad idea," Dunk said as he perched on the edge of his desk. "Tag-team 'em. We can all handle Bull and Todd for a few days at a time."

Jim spoke up. "I'll take 'em."

They all turned and looked at him. Even Thomas couldn't hide his surprise.

Jim shrugged. "I actually want them. Along with Ashley, Clark, and Kenneth. Five person team. The rest of you get six."

Dunk laughed his surprise. "Man, I know you're fucking nuts, but do you have to prove it so early in the session…? I mean, I was expecting some serious crazy from you, but not until around day three…"

"You do have the rep for owning some serious crazy, Spaceman." Lucky used Jim's SEAL-training-acquired nickname as he laughed.

"You actually *want* them, sir...?" Rio couldn't believe it.

"I actually do," Jim answered. "It's gonna be like an afterschool special movie. Everyone's gonna learn the shit out of this."

Lucky was laughing his ass off.

"Learn what?" Dunk asked, starting to laugh, too.

"That... I don't quite know yet," Jim admitted.

Thomas was seriously concerned. "Lieutenant Slade, sir," he started, "since you've never been an instructor here before, I would respectfully suggest—"

"No, no, no, nuh-no, Thomas, don't stop him. This is gonna be *so* much fun to watch," Lucky said, still laughing, but Dunk spoke up over them both.

"You want it?" he asked Jim. "You got it. But if I agree to this, my crazy swim-finned brother, you cannot quit. I own you for the next week. No ringing out."

"Agreed," Jim promised. "I'm here."

Dunk grinned. "Bull's gonna shit bricks and—oh, frabjous day—quite possibly never come back."

"And then," Jim said with a smile, "there's *that*."

Ashley found Clark and Kenneth hunched over the Space Invaders game.

Tonight's dinner had been surprisingly good—a hearty roast chicken with potatoes and carrots, with a spinach and cucumber salad. She had, however, sat alone since her brother and his friend had gotten there early, inhaled their food, and vanished into the lounge.

It was actually interesting the way the other campers avoided eye contact. They looked past her or over her or through her as the tension in their shoulders shouted *Please God, don't let the creature with the vagina be part of my team.*

Once, when she was a kid, she'd stumbled into her older cousin's boy-cave in the basement of his suburban house. She thought she'd merely been going down to the rec room, but instead she'd entered a loudly proclaimed *Boys Only* territory. Shouting and screaming had ensued, and her father had pulled her aside to advise that she be more careful in the future, and not violate their "safe space."

She'd learned to move about more quietly and not call attention to herself. She'd intended to do the same thing here—until she'd found out that she was part of a *team.*

There was no getting around that. She was going to seriously mess-up someone's misogynistic day—unless Jim Slade delivered on his suggestion to create a smaller group with only Ash, Clark, and Kenneth.

Ashley poured herself a glass of wine from an open bottle of a very nice California Pinot Noir. As she started to input her PIN into the iPad attached to the bar, Jim appeared and stopped her.

"Tonight, the first one's on the house," he said, slipping onto the bar stool next to her.

"To help ease the pain?" she asked as she took a sip. The room was filling up around them, and the anticipation and anxiety was palpable. Or maybe she was projecting.

Jim smiled. "It's really not going to be that bad."

For *him,* perhaps… "So how exactly do we do this team-picking thing?" Ashley asked. "Is there a hat, like in *Harry Potter…*? Or is it more like the humiliation of middle school gym class?"

"It's definitely not that," Jim said. "Although a talking hat would be pretty damn cool."

She looked at him. "Books or movies?"

"Both were good, in Harry's case," he said, "but as a general rule, I prefer the written word." He smiled again. "And see, that look…? The one you're giving me—"

"I'm not giving you a look."

"Yeah. You are. You're good at hiding it, but it's back there. It's the *Huh, I took you more for the reality-TV-watching type. In fact, I wasn't sure you even* knew *how to read* look. It comes from having a face like a pugilist."

She took another sip of wine. "Nice word."

"Didn't want to use *boxer* and have you thinking that *I* think I have a face like a dog." He grinned at her. "It's not *that* bad, as far as faces go."

It certainly wasn't, but she would never tell him that. Instead, she hid her smile in her glass of wine.

"As far as how we select the teams," Jim continued, "it's already been done. Dunk's gonna come in and read off the assignments. There's gonna be noise; ignore it if you can—Dunk'll shut it down. We'll then meet in groups to assign a TL—a team leader."

And there came Dunk, into the room followed by Thomas, Rio, and Lucky. Ashley felt her shoulders tense.

"It's gonna be okay," Jim murmured.

Ashley turned to him, unable to stop herself from asking, "Should I have quit?"

He laughed. "Only if you thought it would be fun for me to mock you endlessly."

"Endlessly?" she asked. "I think it would've ended when I left in the morning."

"And I'm pretty sure Dunk has your email address," Jim said. "I definitely would've continued to mock you endlessly from afar."

"Seriously," she said. "I know that Dunk would've made an exception to his no-refund rule for me. My being here *has* to be a challenge for him—and for you and the other instructors, too."

"There's not a Navy SEAL alive who doesn't love a good challenge," Jim pointed out, leaning closer and lowering his voice as the room fell to an anticipatory hush.

"Good evening," Dunk said. "Did everyone enjoy Lieutenant Slade's chicken?"

Ashley turned to see Jim giving a pope-wave and laughed. "*You* cooked that dinner?"

"Such incredulity," he said *sotto voce* as Dunk continued to speak, explaining how he was going to announce the teams, who would then break off into groups to get to know one another.

"Not that you cooked it," Ashley lowered her voice to tell Jim. "It was crazy delicious, by the way—but that you somehow had *time*."

"A man, a plan, and a roaster with a lid," he whispered back. "Or in this case, when feeding thirty-ish people, an abundance of roasters with lids, and a team of sous chefs or grunts as we call 'em in the service—the carrot and potato peelers. I drizzled the olive oil and applied the spices and put the *exact* amount of water in the bottom of the pans. Everything mixed together and… Into the oven for two hours—with that lid, you cannot overcook, you can only make it better. There's time to shower and even attend a meeting or two. Excuse me."

Yes, Dunk *had* just requested his SEAL instructors join him at the front of the room for the team announcements.

As Ashley watched Jim Slade walk across the lounge—trying not to limp—she realized that maybe, just maybe, this next week wasn't going to be as awful as she'd imagined.

She and Jim, along with Clark and Kenneth, might actually have fun and…

Theirs was the first team announced. "Lt. Jim Slade will be instructor for Team One, which includes Ashley DeWitt, Clark DeWitt, Kenneth Price…"

And there it was except, inexplicably, Dunk kept going.

"…Todd Grotto and Dwight "Bull" Edison."

"What…?" Bull put voice to what they all were thinking, his *what* going up several octaves to High-Soprano-Land. "What the *hell*!"

Ashley was too stunned to speak. Todd and Bull were part of their team…? She looked over at Jim, but he was not looking at her, and with a sinking heart she realized his admonishment for her not to quit had probably *not* been entirely honest.

"Settle down there," Dunk said as the men in the room who were not Bull or Todd murmured their relief. "Moving on to Team Two," Dunk announced, but whatever he said after that, Ashley had no idea.

All she could think was, shit… *shit*!

CHAPTER FOUR

Ashley looked shell-shocked.

As Jim watched, she brought her still half-full glass of wine over to the table that he'd decreed as belonging to Team One. She sat down across from him, but the smart, funny woman he'd been talking to at the bar had vanished.

Bull and Todd were in the corner, having a heated but relatively quiet discussion with Dunk.

The three other teams were buzzing with both excitement and relief as they connected at other tables throughout the room.

"Dunk's telling them that because we're a five-man team—the other teams each have six; two campers dropped out this afternoon, so… Anyway, because there's only five of you, he's going to allow me to join you when you compete," Jim explained as Clark and Kenneth sat down, too. "At least until there're more dropouts to even things out."

The two boys—both looking uncharacteristically grim—purposely chose chairs on either side of Ashley, ensuring that neither Todd nor Bull would be able to sit too close to her.

"That's supposed to be a good thing?" Clark asked. "Dude, you hide the limp pretty well, but no one is fooled. Speculation abounds about the extent of your injuries."

Kenneth, surprisingly, defended Jim to Clark. "Still, he's a SEAL. This training is a vacation for him. Our paltry challenges are things he can do with both hands tied behind his back."

Clark turned to his friend. "Yeah, but look at the rest of us. Out of you, me, and Ash, *she's* the most athletic. Add in the rage twins over there…"

Across the room, Dunk was still listening to whatever Very Important Thing Bull was earnestly telling him. One possibility was that both Bull and Todd would decide to go home early. Jim hoped that wouldn't happen—at least not right away.

"Can Lieutenant Slade do our *paltry challenges* with both hands *and* feet tied?" Clark asked Kenneth.

"Whose idea was it?" Ashley suddenly asked. She looked up, directly at Jim.

He knew what she meant—and that she wanted him to say it was Dunk's idea to put Bull and Todd on their team. But he wasn't going to lie. "It was mine."

She nodded. "Okay. Wow. Your apology," she said. "It worked."

Jim didn't understand. "Worked?"

"I was disarmed," she admitted. "I thought... Well, my bad."

"Ho, now," Jim said. "I meant what I said. And *you* said you wanted to learn something."

"I wanted to learn something *new*," she told him, way too evenly. Why wasn't she more visibly upset? She was rather freakishly calm. "I mastered getting my ass grabbed the summer before seventh grade."

And... she wasn't upset because apparently this experience was unfolding exactly as she'd expected it to unfold. Seventh grade was twelve, thirteen years old... Holy shit. "Boys can be idiots," Jim started.

"These weren't boys," she informed him coolly. "They were grown men. Friends of my father's. I learned to keep my distance."

Christ. "You should've learned to tell someone—"

"Believe me, I did." She took another sip of her wine. "I also learned that no one cares."

"I care," Jim said.

She laughed. "You sure have a funny way of showing it."

"You could quit," he pointed out.

"I could," Ashley agreed.

"Incoming," Kenneth murmured, and they both looked up to see that Bull and Todd had finished their conversation with Dunk and were stomping toward their table.

"Brace yourself for impact," Clark muttered, "in three, two..."

"Team One," Bull said, putting his glass of beer down on the table with so much force that the amber liquid sloshed over the sides. He looked directly at Ashley. "We'll have to make the best of this, won't we?"

She looked over to see Lieutenant Slade—their team instructor—watching her steadily from across the table.

"The girl and the gay dudes," Todd said with a scornful laugh as he sat down. He was a slightly smaller, thinner version of Bull.

"Thank you, but... we're not gay," Kenneth said. "We're just..."

"Hipsters?" Todd asked. "That's pretty gay."

"A)" Lieutenant Slade said in a tone that brooked no argument, "we will not use *gay* as a pejorative. And B) Ashley is a woman. Show some respect."

Bull was still standing, and he grabbed his crotch as he told Ashley, "I got some steaming hot respect for you right here, sweetheart."

"Enough. Sit. *Now*," Slade ordered.

Bull sat but he still made kissing noises in Ashley's direction.

And again, the SEAL was looking at her, as if waiting for her to do something.

But Ashley had found that nothing worked better than refusal to engage. Ignore and avoid. Although avoiding Bull was going to be impossible, since they were on the same team... That left *ignore*, so she calmly took another sip of her wine.

Lieutenant Slade finally spoke. "Okay. Let's go around the table, introduce ourselves—where you're from, what you do, and what you hope to gain from this session. Kenneth, why don't you start?"

"Oh, uh, yes, of course," Kenneth said. "Kenneth Price. Originally from the UK, little town just outside of London... College student, Boston University, English major... Hoping to gain... I want to say... life experience...?"

"Good. Thank you. How about you, Clark?" the SEAL prompted.

"Clark DeWitt. I'm Ashley's brother and Kenneth's roommate. Originally from New York. I'm here because I'd... well, I was thinking of maybe trying to become a SEAL someday."

Ashley looked at him. She'd had no idea... "Really?"

Bull snorted his disdain. "*That'll* never happen."

Ashley shot him a hard look. "You don't know that." She turned to Clark. "I think that's a great aspiration."

"I think you mean *pipe dream*," Bull said.

"I think you need to zip it," she shot back at him.

"I know one way you can get me to *zip it*," he said. "Although it starts with *unzipping* a different *it*."

Nope, not going there. Ashley looked at their SEAL instructor, who again was looking back at her. "May we continue? I'll go next. I'm Ashley DeWitt. From San Felipe, California—it's near San Diego. I'm a lawyer for a family law practice that specializes in protecting women who are victims of domestic violence."

Bull laughed. "Of course you are."

"I hope to gain... confidence," Ash said.

Bull grabbed himself again. "I got a confidence injection for you right here, baby-cakes," he said.

Clark had had enough. "You know, you read as pathetic," he told Bull. "You're not funny, you're just stupid and ignorant—"

As Bull bristled, Ashley leaned slightly against her brother. "It's okay," she murmured. "Just... pretend he's not here."

"Does that really work?" Lieutenant Slade asked. He was still watching her. He'd been watching her since this gathering had started. No doubt ready for her to quit and walk away. "Because in my experience... well, I've never been able to just wish an adversary away."

"Can we finish here?" she asked in response. "I'd like to get back to my camper. I'm still working on my recovery from my jet-lag."

"We need to elect a team leader," Bull pointed out. "In fact, I nominate Ashley."

"I second it," his friend Todd said.

And before Ash could begin to form the N for *no*, Kenneth and Clark, not realizing what they were doing, chimed in with "Third!" and "Fourth!"

"Good, so that's decided," Bull said with a smirk. "You'll get a packet of info that tells you what you have to do—it's mostly just taking attendance, and bringing us coffee in the morning."

What? Ashley looked at Lieutenant Slade, who was shaking his head. "No, to the coffee, but yes to the packet," he said.

"Yeah, but lowest scoring team member has to bring the morning coffee," Bull pointed out. "Since that's gonna be her, anyways..." He smiled at her. "I was trying to give you an out, TL—that stands for team leader. If I had to choose between bringing coffee because I was team leader, or because I sucked..."

"I'll bring the coffee," the lieutenant said.

Bull shrugged. "Sir, yes, sir! And now I suppose I should do the intro thing, even though I'm pretty sure you all know who I am. Bull Edison, from Indianapolis, Indiana. Assistant manager of finance and sales at a Fortune Five Hundred company that shall remain unnamed. This is the third time I've come to camp. This time I'm hoping for a balls-deep experience."

He was looking right at her, so Ashley instead focused on her wine glass, hoping he was done.

He wasn't. "I mean, I really wanna *plough* my way through the next two weeks, go at this thing *hard* and *rough* and—"

"Thank you," Lieutenant Slade interrupted him. "Todd?"

Todd worked with Bull, and he was looking to improve his paintball game score.

Paintball. Great. Ashley was going to suck at paintball.

"Well, since you seem to have come to an agreement about your team leader..." the SEAL lieutenant said, again as he looked at Ashley, as if waiting for... what?

She was certain that being team leader was going to be awful— confirmation coming in that packet of info—but if it wasn't her, then who? No way was she subjecting Clark and Kenneth to Team Leader Todd or—God help them—Bull.

"We voted," Todd said. "The chick's it."

"I do believe we are done here," Bull said. "Boom. Bull out!"

He and Todd laughed as they got up and walked away.

Ashley stood, too. She had to get out of there—God forbid she start to cry. "I'll see you guys in the morning."

Jim followed Ashley out of the mess hall and into the heat of the Florida night. Tropical insects were making a racket in the trees, and the air was thick and humid. "Wait up. I'll walk you."

"You don't have to." She barely glanced at him. Her voice was calm but her shoulders were tight.

"We're going in the same direction."

"Yes," she said with the slightest of sighs. "I noticed that I was assigned the RV between yours and Lieutenant King's. That wasn't necessary. I don't need protection."

"You sure?" Jim asked. "Because that was pretty passive back there. I kept waiting for you to do something, and you just didn't." He'd purposely tried not to step in—although a few times Bull pushed him too far. Still, he'd waited and waited and *waited* for Ashley to defend herself. But she hadn't.

She finally looked over at him, her face a pale blur in the mostly-moonlight that lit their way, but again her voice was even. "I'm sorry, you think my being *passive* is the problem...? Not Bull's language and behavior...?"

"So you *do* want my protection," he countered.

Ashley laughed a little. "That's not what I said."

"Isn't it?" he poked. She had to be furious with him, or at the very least massively, crushingly disappointed, but aside from the tightness in her shoulders, she let none of that show. And, in fact, as he looked more closely at her body language, her tension seemed to be more about bracing for another attack than righteously brittle anger.

As they approached her RV, she ignored his question as deftly as she'd ignored Bull and Todd back in the lounge. "Please don't walk me to the door. I'd prefer no one mistake your misguided chivalry for impropriety."

He stopped there, at the fork in the trail. "Although that would be one sure way of convincing Bull and Todd to keep their distance."

She looked at him sharply, and he realized that she'd misunderstood, and quickly added, "I'm not suggesting we actually, um, hook up. That wouldn't be... No. I mean, the *implication* would be an easy solution. Just to make them *think* that—"

She cut him off. "*That's* your idea of a solution?"

Jim shrugged. "They're Neanderthals. It would work. Put a little fear into 'em."

"Fear of *you*," she pointed out.

"Yeah, sorry, I don't think they're ever going to fear you," he told her.

"I'm not looking for fear," Ashley said. "Just respect."

"I get it," he said. "But I doubt you'll be able to change them."

"*Boys will be boys...?*" she said.

"Sadly, yes. I mean, I don't agree with that, of course, but that's how the world works."

She surprised him then. "I don't accept that it can't be changed."

"Then you're going to have to do more than ignore them," Jim told her. "It's an uphill battle—wow, we are just dropping the clichés, here, aren't we?"

Ashley smiled, but only because she was polite. "It's uphill, because the idea—the massively offensive idea—that a woman needs to belong to a man so that she's treated with respect is acceptable to, well, *you*. If you really believe that, you're a part of the problem. Think about your suggestion—and what it really means. A woman on her own is fair game to idiots like Bull, but he'll back off if he thinks someone else possesses her. But he's not treating *her* with respect. No, the respect is man to man—right over the head of the woman. *I won't treat your woman like shit out of deference to you, Brah.*"

Jesus. He'd never considered... Still, "That's a pretty good imitation of Bull, but I don't think *deference* is in his vocabulary."

Frustration flared in her eyes, but just for a very brief moment before she tamped it back down. "Good night, Lieutenant," she said, heading for her RV.

"You know, sometimes it's okay to get pissed off," he called after her.

"And do what? Kick you in the shins? That's really not my style."

"As opposed to running and hiding?" he said.

His words struck a nerve—she practically flinched. But when she turned back, her voice stayed even and calm. "I'm tired—it's been a long day. I'm sure we'll have plenty of time to continue this discussion, because sorry, but I'm not quitting."

"I'm not even close to sorry about that," Jim said. "No one here wants you to quit. Well, those of us who aren't Bull and Todd."

But she laughed again, just a little, and he knew she didn't believe him. "Good night," she said again.

And as Jim watched, she used the keypad to unlock her door, and went inside, not looking back.

CHAPTER FIVE

Ashley awoke with a start. Someone was pounding on her door, shouting, "Team Leader DeWitt!"

Was it really morning already? But it was still pitch dark.

She grabbed for her phone in the darkness, to use the light from the screen to get her bearings, first to figure out where she was—SEAL World—and then to realize that whoever was pounding wasn't hammering on the flimsy door but rather the side of the RV.

Also…? It was barely midnight.

She found the switch that turned on the interior LEDs, and pushed her hair back from her face as she unlocked the door and opened it a crack.

The young SEAL named Rio Rosetti was standing out there. "Good morning, ma'am," he said in his almost-ridiculously stereotypical New Yawk accent.

Ash stared at him stupidly. The best her brain could come up with was, "Are you delivering my team leader packet?"

He'd been all smiles and even a bit flirty when they'd first met, but now he was all curt business. "No, ma'am. Hat, and boots if you got 'em, long pants, long sleeves, leave all technology behind. Team leaders're meeting down by the mess in five, but you've already wasted two sleeping through my noise, so you got three. Tick tock. Ma'am."

She closed the door and took several of her precious minutes to use the bathroom, then dressed quickly, slipping into jeans and pulling a lightweight button down shirt on over the T-shirt she'd worn to bed. She didn't have boots—she'd brought a second pair of running shoes instead, and she jammed her bare feet into them. Her Red Sox cap was hanging directly in front of the AC vent—she'd sweated through it yesterday, and had rinsed it out right before bed.

She reached for it as Rio again started pounding on the RV, but it was still soaking wet.

"Time to go!"

There were SEAL World hats—boonie style—in the Gedunk.

She'd been meaning to get one anyway. She could pick one up there, so she left her cap hanging, turned off the lights, and went out of the RV, checking that the door locked securely behind her.

Now Rio was clapping his hands at her, rather like she was a misbehaving puppy, so she headed toward the mess hall at a run.

Only to find the passenger van idling, headlights sending beams of brightness into the steamy humidity of the night. In the distance, thunder rumbled.

"Let's go, let's go, let's go!" Lieutenant Slade was standing by the van's door, and he opened it and motioned for her to get inside.

"Wait," she said, stopping short. "What?" She pointed ineffectively toward the mess hall as the lieutenant herded her up and into the van.

Ashley wasn't quite sure how he did it without touching her, but before she could say *hat*, she was inside and sitting, and he'd pulled himself up and in, too, closing the door behind him to take the seat beside her.

She'd only had a few brief moments to look around before the interior light went off with the closing of the door, but it had been long enough to get a full dose of smug impatience from the three other team leaders, who'd been waiting for her.

It seemed unlikely that they'd all woken up and gotten down here to the van in less than five minutes, and she realized that Rio had probably intentionally pounded on her RV last.

Probably on Dunk or even Lieutenant Slade's orders.

But she had other things to worry about right now—like, where were they going?

All of the SEAL instructors were in the van, too. Including the medic—what was it called in Navy-Speak...? The *hospital corpsman*, Thomas King.

Dunk was behind the wheel, and as Rio climbed into the front passenger seat the vehicle moved out of the parking area and onto the long drive that led from the camp to the road.

The van lurched as they hit a pothole, and Ashley found herself pressed up against Lieutenant Slade's shoulder. He looked down at her, his face even more craggy in the shadows, his eyes a flash of blue. She murmured, "Sorry," and tried to steady herself by holding on to the seat back in front of her.

"For those of us, like, me, who are new here," Slade then said loudly, as if he were addressing everyone in the van, "we're heading out on the traditional night hike. Team leaders are paired up with team instructors, but it's the TL's job to lead the march back to camp. Dunk's gonna drop us about five miles out—"

"Five *miles*?" Ashley murmured before she could stop herself.

But Lieutenant Slade spoke over her. "Like everything from this point on at SEAL World, it's a race. First team in gets a head start on every activity over the next two days, which allows that team to continue to come in first and gain advantages for the entire week," he continued. "Last team in gets literal shit—black tank evac duty for the RVs and trailers. For those of you who are RV-unfamiliar, the black tank is the one in your trailer that your toilet flushes into. And trust me, emptying black tanks is *not* fun."

Dunk spoke up. "We'll be dropping you with your instructor in the order in which you arrived in the van."

Ashley laughed. Of course. She and Jim Slade would be dropped last.

"It's likely that some of you will get very lost," Dunk continued, "since we're giving you neither a map nor a compass and it's dark out there. If after three hours, you haven't made it back to camp, we'll find you via a GPS tracker that you'll be given when you leave the van. Winners and losers will be determined by their distance from the camp. Farther from camp, the bigger the loser, so... good luck."

Ashley looked at Lieutenant Slade who was watching her again. "Do instructors help with the black-tank-emptying thing...?" she whispered.

He laughed and shook his head. "Not a chance."

"Put on your hat," Jim ordered as he handed Ashley some bug repellent wipes as the van's taillights faded into the night.

"Um," she said.

He held his flashlight overhead so that it lit both of their faces. And yes, the resigned look she was giving him was heavily tinged with *No, I didn't bring my hat.*

"Seriously?" he said. It was going to rain—at night, in this part of Florida, that was inevitable. And that was going to suck even worse for anyone without a hat brim to shield their face.

"My lack of hat isn't our biggest problem," she told him as she used the light to read the directions on the packet before tearing one open and rubbing the wipe down the sleeves of her shirt and the legs of her jeans. "It's the five miles—more than that, if we go in the wrong direction."

"I don't know why you think that's a problem," Jim answered. "You can walk *ten* miles, easily, if you have to."

"I can *run* ten miles," she responded with a tartness that was refreshing. "In fact, I call that *Tuesday evening after work*. It's not me I'm worried about—it's you."

Jim was surprised. "Me?"

"Yes, Mr. Braces-on-Both-Knees," Ashley said. "I'm worried about *you*."

"Well, don't be," Jim said brusquely. "Five miles is nothing."

"More if we go the wrong way," she reminded him.

"Then don't go the wrong way," he countered.

"No map," she reminded him. "No compass." She looked up at the sky, which tended to be hazy in the humid tropics, even at the best of times. Now, however, thunder rumbled ominously in the distance. "No stars to follow, assuming I could even find the north star with all these trees. Assuming I also knew if we were north—or south or whatever—of the camp."

The narrow sand-and-gravel road they were standing on was surrounded by a mix of pines, palms, and banyan trees, the latter with their vast collection of trunks that started out as curling vines snaking down from broadly-spread branches to take root in the earth below.

This would've been a relatively pleasant place to hike—in the daylight. Assuming the overpowering smell of dead-fish-hiding-somewhere-in-a-damp-locker-room faded in the sunshine.

Ashley turned to look down the road in the direction they'd approached while still in the van. "If we follow the road back that way, we'll eventually get to the camp," she said, obviously thinking out loud. "Except we made so many turns and stops and... I'm pretty sure we went in a big circle. And the van left going *that* way." She pointed down the road where the van had vanished. "So there must be *some*thing down there..."

Jim waited as she looked back down the road in the other direction, clearly undecided.

"Do you have another flashlight?" she finally asked, turning to focus her gaze on him.

"No, they only gave me this one." Hint, hint. *Gave me.* Jim knew Ashley had a very big brain. She just had to wake up enough to use it.

"Okay," she said with a sigh, "you better keep it then. But turn it off for a sec, so my eyes can get used to the dark."

Jim had to wonder about that *you better keep it*—what was she thinking...? Still, he obliged and they were plunged into the kind of moonless darkness that was suffocating in its absoluteness. It descended around him, heavy and wet against the bare skin of his face and hands.

Ashley must've been having the same reaction. "Shhhhhit," she breathed, the word barely voiced.

"Let your eyes get used to it." His own voice was a rumble in his chest as his other senses kicked in more fully. There was a raucous battle going on between tree frogs and locusts, and Team Locust was winning.

He could hear the sound of Ashley breathing, too. Her inhales were too shallow—she was breathing too fast.

"Easy," he murmured.

"Nothing about any of this is easy," she muttered.

"Rumor has it that Bull Edison wept and wet himself before *his* team leader night-hike was over," Jim told her.

She laughed. "Telling me that is inappropriate. And mean."

"Or I'm creating a false narrative to bolster your self-confidence."

This time her laughter was a short burst of air but no less musical. "You mean you're lying to keep *me* from weeping and wetting myself."

"I'm convinced that weeping and wetting yourself is something that you would never do. Ever," he emphasized as his own eyes adjusted and she turned into a dark shape standing on the road beside him.

But she sighed heavily again. "This isn't going to work," Ashley said.

"What isn't?"

"I thought I could run ahead—leave you here with the flashlight. I thought if I could move fast, I could see where this road leads—if it's an obvious route back to the camp—and then run back to let you know if I'm right. But there's no way I can run without a light. This darkness is dizzying."

"So take the flashlight," he suggested.

"I'm not leaving you alone in the dark."

"Navy SEAL," he pointed out.

"I don't care," she said.

"Really, Ashley, I've been left alone in the dark a *lot*."

"Well, I'm not gonna do that to you. Not tonight." She was absolute, which was interesting. Apparently she *was* capable of standing her ground—when someone else's comfort and safety were at risk.

He heard more than saw her shift, but was still surprised when her fingers lightly bumped his shoulder.

"Sorry," she quickly said.

Jesus. If someone followed this woman around and recorded everything she ever said, the word-cloud created would feature *Sorry* smack in the middle, in a size four hundred font.

She cleared her throat. "May I have... Are you allowed to let me have the flashlight? You *did* say I could take it...?"

"Here. Yes." Jim caught her reaching hand and pressed her fingers around the thing, making sure she had it firmly in her grasp before he let it and her go. Funny, her fingers were cool despite the night's heat. Cool but not as fairy-princess soft as he'd imagined. She clearly used her hands to do hard work. Huh.

"Thanks," she said. "Watch your eyes, Lieutenant, I'm turning it on."

The fact that she'd thought to give him a heads-up was interesting, too. Dunk had given Jim and the other the instructors a variety of warnings about working with civilians, and the most dire involved the use of NVGs—night vision goggles. *Be ready*, the former senior chief had said, *for some numbnuts to flip on the headlights and completely blind you.*

Apparently, Ashley DeWitt didn't fall into the typical SEAL World *numbnuts* subset.

And yet again, she was surprising Jim as he watched her through squinted eyes. He'd expected her to lead the way down the road in the direction that the van had driven off—at a walking pace so that he and his freaking knee braces could keep up. Instead she used the beam of the light to explore the area at the side of the road. She even shone the light up into the branches of a big banyan tree.

He laughed, and she glanced over at him so he said, "I have no idea what you're looking for."

"It's going to rain," she informed him as—right on cue—thunder rumbled. And yes, it was louder—the storm was closer—this time. "I was hoping this tree would provide at least a little shelter."

"Shelter...?" Jim echoed.

She used the light to examine a rather impressive lump of a bench-sized tree root before somewhat gingerly sitting down on it.

"What...?" Jim laughed. "Wait..."

"Exactly," she said, looking up at him. "That's my plan. We wait."

He found himself pointing down the road. "You don't want to...?"

"Potentially put more miles between us and the camp?" she finished his question for him. "Nope."

Now he was surprised for a different reason. "Wow, I didn't peg you as a quitter."

"I didn't say *quit*," Ashley said. "I said *wait*. We *know* we're five miles from the camp, and we also know the GPS will go off in three hours. I'm banking on the fact that at least *one* of the other team leaders will go crashing off in the wrong direction and put himself more than five miles from the camp, which means that his team—not mine—will win the black-tank loser's prize."

"Sitting still means you definitely won't win the, you know, *winner's* prize," Jim pointed out.

"Please sit down," she told him. "I'm turning off the flashlight, both to conserve batteries and to keep mosquitos from being drawn to us."

As he sat, she plunged them back into darkness as she continued, "I feel pretty confident that the winner's prize is not within our reach. Realistically. I mean, come on. But not-losing—not coming in dead last—*that* we can do. With a little luck. Especially when that also means *you* don't have to walk *any* miles tonight."

"You need to stop worrying about me. I'll be fine."

He heard her turn toward him, even though he was surely as much of a dark faceless shape to her as she was to him. She asked, "You really expect me to believe that your knees won't hurt after five miles—"

"My fucking knees hurt," Jim snapped, "every fucking minute of my fucking life, regardless of whether I'm sitting still or walking."

And... scene.

Except there was no curtain, and the frogs and locusts were still screaming their relentless chorus with that basso profundo thunder descant coming more often now. Could a descant be basso profundo, or did it always have to be a soprano line? Jim honestly didn't know and he filed it under *Things he'd Google later, when he was back in his RV icing his knees.*

Meanwhile, Ashley's silent response to his bratty baby-man outburst continued to rack up time on this conversation's scoreboard.

When she finally spoke, it was to say, "I'm so sorry."

"Oh, *Jesus!*" Her use of her favorite word pissed him off all over again. "You don't have to be sorry for *my* freaking knees! What you *should* be sorry for is your bullshit acceptance of some deluded belief that just because you're a girl you can't win this thing!"

She countered his loud-and-angry with a voice that was super calm and in control. "I'm a woman, not a girl."

"Yeah, no, *sorry*," he said. "How did you say it?" He spoke in an obnoxiously bad imitation of a high-pitched little girl's voice, complete with an Elmer Fudd-like speech impediment. *"A wittle girl like me will never win a game against all those big stwong boys. Wealistically. I'm just too weak and dumb. I mean, come on."* Back to his real voice. "What the hell was *that*...? You know what you don't have? You don't have upper body strength. Big deal. You have a giant brain and legs that can run forever—"

"And a companion who just admitted he's in constant pain—which I already knew. I could tell just from looking at your face," she said, but her voice was still calm, contained. "That was me, doing what I *thought* a team leader was supposed to do—be aware of my teammate's limitations. Because I also know that you're lying, and your knees *will* hurt worse after walking five miles. I said *we* couldn't win this thing, but if I were alone, trust me, I would already be running."

"Then run," he said. "I'll keep up."

"No," she said. "But I will let you sit here in the dark. Flashlight's going on," she warned as she stood up. "Move into the road. I'm going to run out about a mile, and then I'll come back. It'll take me about fifteen minutes."

Jim stood, too. "Yeah, I can't let you do that. There's really only one unbreakable rule for this particular exercise. Separation of team leader and instructor is that one giant no-can-do."

Ashley stared at him in disbelief.

He shrugged and hit her with her favorite word. "Sorry."

It was then, with diabolical timing, that thunder clapped almost directly overhead, and the skies opened up in a deluge.

CHAPTER SIX

"You told me to take the flashlight," Ashley shouted at Jim over the roar of the rain as he pulled her closer to the main trunk of the banyan tree. "You tried to talk me into leaving you here! And now that's *not an option...*?"

The branches overhead helped only a little, and she had to close her eyes because the rain was streaming down her face. Without a hat, it was like standing in the bathtub with her face aimed up at the shower head.

"It was actually a good idea," he shouted back. "I wanted to see if you'd do it. And since you didn't want to, I didn't have to shut it down. Until you did, and then I did. Shut you down. Because yeah, we've gotta stay together. We can definitely run—I *can* keep up."

Ashley opened her eyes to look at him and had to use her hands to shield her face from the rain. "You're serious."

He was still holding the flashlight and it made his eyes look very blue. "Yeah. Navy SEAL...?"

It was then, as their gazes were locked with the rain pouring down around them and on top of them that Ashley realized... She may not have had a map, but she had a *Navy SEAL*.

"What would you do?" she asked him. "If you were in charge."

"First, it's called command, *if I were in command*."

"That," she said. "What would you do?"

He was silent but only for a few seconds before he said, "I'd take inventory."

"Inventory?" she repeated.

"Yeah, you know, what do I have, what do you have...?" he said. "I'd also do an inventory of the team members' skill sets. You're a runner, that's great, but alas, right now I'm an anti-runner, with my knees. But okay, what *else* are you good at? Arguing a court case—not gonna do us a helluva lot of good out here..."

"What are *your* skill sets?" Ashley asked him. "An ability to pull an extra baseball cap out of your ass during a thunderstorm would be awesome."

Jim laughed. "Okay, so *you're* way funnier than I thought."

"What," she repeated as pleasantly as she could, "are your skills sets?"

"Are you sure that's the question you want to start with?" he countered.

Ashley rewound their conversation just a bit and... "What are you carrying in your pockets or... wherever... that could help us? I have the GPS tracker thing that'll let them find us, and basically my clothes and underwear, although right now I'm desperately wishing I took the time to put on a bra. You have... a flashlight... What else?"

His gaze had flickered down to her chest at *bra*, but her arms were crossed because the rain was chilling. And also because her shirt and PJ top were both white and probably transparent while soaking wet.

"Here," he said, shrugging out of it. "Take my over-shirt."

"What I really want is your ass-cap."

He laughed again. "Sorry. No extra hat, or... ass-pulling-out-of hat-producing skill-set."

"That's too bad." She took his shirt gratefully. It was heavier than hers—more like a jacket than a shirt—and still warm from his body heat. "So what else do you have with you?"

"A power bar," he told her. "And... drum roll, please... my phone."

She gasped. Oh my God! "You have your *phone*? Are we allowed to use it?" She answered her own question. "Yes, because there's only one rule—that we stick together. So, hand it over— wait! Does it have a water resistant case?" God forbid she got him to hand over his phone, only to have it drown in the ongoing deluge.

Jim was grinning broadly at her. "Navy SEAL," he said. "And congratulations—"

"Hold the champagne, and be less cryptic," she ordered.

"SEAL stands for Sea, Air, Land," he said, still smiling as he handed her his unlocked phone, "so yes, my case is water*proof* not just resistant. It's not dive-proof, though."

"*Not* planning to scuba dive any time soon, thanks," Ashley told him, already manipulating the screen through the plastic cover. He had great cell connection—a surprising full set of bars out here in the middle of nowhere—so she scrolled through his applications to find a map with GPS, and the fastest, shortest route back to camp.

"Brains over brawn," Jim said. "We just might win this thing."

They didn't win.

But they placed, coming in second, which was significantly better than Bull had done a few months back, when he'd done his Team Leader Night Hike.

Or so Jim had heard.

"Thank you again," Ashley said, handing him his shirt—still soaking wet—as he'd walked her to the fork in the path leading to their separate RVs.

And yeah, the long-sleeved, button-down shirt she was wearing beneath it was white and glued to her body like she'd inadvertently entered some super creepy corporate version of a wet-T-shirt contest. *Don't look, don't look...* Ah, shit, he'd looked, and it was something he could never un-see, because yes, she was female and kinda freaking perfect in a way that was weird, because he generally liked breasts in the XXL range, and hers were far from that.

But Jim now kept his gaze glued to her face—even though it was shadowed by the new boonie she'd picked up at the Gedunk. He had to clear his throat before his vocal chords would work. "You did good."

She recognized that her costume had, indeed, malfunctioned exactly as she'd predicted it would, probably due to his insanely intense eye contact, and awkwardly folded her arms across her chest. "With your help. It seems a little unfair that *you* have to be up by six, too."

Jim checked his watch. It was just after 0330. And he still had to talk to Dunk... "We get a bit of a break, since our first session's on the paintball field."

"*Paintball...?*" And yes, that was dismay in her voice.

"Don't worry, we don't start with a game. That's not scheduled until later in the day. It's good," he tried to reassure her. "It's a learning session. A lot of sitting and listening. Some target practice. But no running or jumping."

"Just Bull and Todd clutching weapons of death in their sweaty, misogynistic hands."

He laughed. "I wouldn't call a paintball marker a weapon of death. A weapon of humiliation, maybe. Still, bravo. Ability to joke at oh-dark-thirty is a highly rated skill in the SpecOp community."

"I wasn't joking," she said, but she did manage to smile back at him. And damn, that smile lit her up. Even wet and bedraggled, she was prettier than most of the women on the planet—at least the ones he'd bumped into in his life. He was lucky they'd spent most of their one-on-one time tonight in pitch darkness. And he was lucky, too, that their being alone together was unlikely to happen again. Which should have made him feel relieved, but didn't, damn it.

"Get some sleep," he said abruptly because the silence had turned slightly odd and charged with... Nope. Not going there. No, no, no. "You did a good job tonight."

"Thanks." Ashley finally turned and headed toward her RV, but then turned back. "Your knees—"

He cut her short, forcing a smile. "No worries, I'm fine."

She was looking at him hard, so he pushed his smile wider. *Fine, see?* She nodded, but he knew she didn't buy it.

"See you in the morning, TL," Jim tossed over his shoulder as he headed back down the trail to the main building.

He tried not to make it obvious, but he watched until she was safely inside of her trailer. Once the door had firmly closed though, he picked up his pace—as well as let himself limp.

Fine—like that crazy-eyed cartoon dog sitting as the room burned around him....

The mess was dark when he got there, but a light was shining from the open door of Dunk's office.

Rio was sprawled—yawning—on the sofa, along with Lucky who was frowning at something he was reading on his phone.

"He here?" Jim asked, *he* being the senior chief—Dunk.

"He's back in the medical supply closet, with his majesty, King Thomas," Lucky looked up to say. He was one of a very few people who dared to tease Thomas—he'd first met the young SEAL officer back when the kid was still in high school—but even he didn't push too hard or far. In a community filled with nicknames—Lucky's real name was Luke, Rio came from Mario, and Jim got called his unfortunate moniker *Spaceman* far more often than he liked—*Thomas* usually wasn't even shortened to Tom or Tommy.

He was respected that enormously. Even in a squad made up of the best of the best, Thomas King was recognized as being elite.

"Hey, LT." Thomas appeared from the back room, carrying a bucket of ice, along with some other gear, including towels and a heating pad.

"Uh-oh, did someone get hurt tonight?" Jim asked.

"Nah, I was gathering this stuff for you, sir."

"Me?"

"Your team leader asked me to get you set up with some ice—and heat, too, if you want it," Thomas told him.

His team leader...? When had Ashley...? Ah, Jim had come out of the head to see her talking quietly with the hospital corpsman, soon after they'd arrived back in the mess hall, right after she'd bought that new hat.

"I'm fine," Jim said again, and it made him think about that word-cloud he'd imagined, and Ashley's *Sorry. His* size-four-hundred-font phrase would be *I'm fine.*

Jesus.

"Yes, sir," Thomas agreed evenly. "But your TL thought a little ice might move you from *fine* to *a little more comfortable.*"

"Then she should've asked you to bring me a cold beer, too," Jim quipped.

Thomas smiled as he pushed a bit of the ice aside to reveal a bottle of Sam Adams nestled in the middle of the bucket. "She appears to be a step ahead of you, sir."

And for once Jim didn't have a smart-ass response, so he just said, "She does."

"I'll walk you back, sir," Thomas said.

"You really don't have to. I can carry my own ice bucket," Jim tried.

As expected, Thomas wouldn't take his *no.* "I'm going that way." He started out the door before Jim could tell him that he needed to talk to Dunk.

But it was Lucky who spoke first. "Oh, hey, Space," he said. "Your team's at the paintball field in the A.M., right? And you've got the O-course after lunch, before our two teams meet for a late session paintball game...?"

Dunk had posted the schedule on a white board that was hanging right there on the wall, so Jim's response was unnecessary. Instead, he simply waited.

"I'm trying to change Team Three's schedule for the morning," Lucky continued. "And I thought I had it worked out with Rio and Team Two, but it'll only work if you guys—Team One—flip your first two sessions to O in the A.M., and paintball instruction after lunch. You mind if we…?"

"Hell, yeah, I mind," Jim said. "My TL earned herself the easier morning."

"Yeah, I'm sorry, you're right, she did." The blond-haired SEAL immediately backed down.

Rio, however, spoke up, telling Jim, "Syd sent him a *We need to talk* email, but her only free time tomorrow is at eleven-hundred, pacific time, which is fourteen-hundred here, and cell signal up at the range is for shit. That's where Lucky's currently slotted. So if you flip *your* times, and I flip *my* times, then he can be at the O-course in the afternoon, where the cell signal is great."

Despite never having been being married, Jim knew that a formal request for serious conversation from one's wife was never good. He looked from Rio to Lucky, who was shaking his head.

"It's really not as dire as it sounds," Lucky said. "We're good. We're *really* good. But Syd's at this writer's conference—that's why her schedule's so tight—and I'm guessing she's been offered another ghost-writing assignment that'll require some insane amount of travel for some ridiculously tiny amount of pay."

Thomas came more completely back into the room. "She can't talk right now, sir? It's not *that* late in California."

"Nah, she's been dealing with some kind of weird food poisoning for the past week," Lucky said. "She ate a taco that just won't leave her system. It's been relentless, so she went to bed early."

"Food poisoning as in, throwing up?" Thomas asked.

Lucky nodded. "Yeah, just when she thinks it's better, it's back. She's exhausted."

"Oh. Wow. Um, sir, that doesn't sound like any kind of food poisoning that I know," Thomas pointed out. "I mean, maybe it's a stomach bug, but…"

"Ah, shit," Jim said on a sigh as he realized what Thomas was implying. Throwing up, exhausted… "Yeah, we'll switch times, so you can talk to Syd without any interference."

Lucky was clueless. "Thanks, but I'll email her and we'll find another time to—"

Even Rio had connected the dots. "By any chance does she puke in the morning and feel a little better in the afternoon?" he asked.

And now Lucky laughed. "Wait, what, you *seriously* don't think…?"

"The *taco that won't leave her system*," Rio repeated, snickering. "I think, sir, that this particular taco might need a name, and help learning to drive when it turns sixteen…"

"Holy shit." Lucky looked as if he didn't know whether to laugh or cry.

"I don't even need to ask my TL," Jim told the SEAL. "I know for a fact she'd say *yes* to the switch."

"And I'll make sure I'm near the O-course in the afternoon," Thomas added. "I'll keep an extra eye on your team while you talk to Syd and, you know, pick out a name. If it's a girl, Thomasina's way underused."

"Yeah, for a reason." Rio snorted as they all laughed.

"Congratulations." Jim held out his hand to Lucky, who pulled back in mock horror.

"Not yet," he said. "Don't jinx it."

"So… this… *taco*… is a good thing, sir…?" Rio asked.

"Damn straight," Lucky said, laughing even as he surreptitiously wiped his eyes. "We've both wanted this for a long time. Syd just started researching the whole hormone thing, you know, where she gives herself injections and then we have to have sex at the exact right nano-second, and that was going to be hard because I just can't come home at any time, like I could if I worked in an office, so I was actually thinking I'd have to resign my—"

"No!" Thomas and Rio said at the same time.

"I hear you, but… Guys, I really want a baby. I want to make a family with Syd," Lucky told them with a shrug. "I love her more than life, and she really wants this, too. You tadpoles are adorable, but let's face it, changing *your* diapers is just not the same."

And yeah, everyone laughed, but Jim was struck by the concept that happy-go-lucky Lieutenant Luke O'Donlon wanted a *baby*, apparently even more than he wanted to remain an active-duty U.S. Navy SEAL.

"Leaving the Teams just isn't as bad as you think it'll be, back when you're in your twenties." Dunk had come out from the back room, and yeah, he was looking at Thomas and Rio, but he was really talking to Jim.

Except Jim didn't have a long-held secret desire to travel the world to see art museums, or to have a baby, Jesus save him. He didn't even have anyone in his life that he loved even a small fraction as much as Lucky loved his wife.

Although, weirdly, the image of Ashley's expressive eyes beneath the brim of that boonie flashed crazily through his mind.

She was attracted to him, too—he'd been alive long enough to recognize that something-something in a woman's attitude and body language.

But really, she was little more than another shiny, pretty thing that he could acquire for a while. A woman like Ashley DeWitt would never stand for being second to anyone or anything for very long.

And Jim's own devotion, for well over a decade, had been to the SEAL Teams. But the Teams didn't always love you back, especially when your knees started to go. And the truly sad thing was that his constant focus on his knees had put distance between himself and his teammates. In fact, because he'd spent so much time over the past few years away from the units, rehabbing, he doubted he'd get the same resounding *no* to *his* announcement he was leaving that Lucky had just received from Team Ten's younger members.

And wah-wah-wah, he himself was such a freaking baby. Still, try as he might to shake off the bitterness of his envy and frustration, it just seemed to settle and solidify into a brick of sadness, smack in the center of his chest.

In the positive, it gave him something to focus on other than the constant pain in his knees.

"You need me for something, Space?" Dunk asked Jim, who shook his head.

"Nah, it can wait 'til tomorrow," he told the Senior Chief. He'd wanted to talk about Ashley, but not in front of a crowd. "Oh, except O'Donlon, Rosetti, and I are adjusting the schedule a bit, so he can talk to Syd in the early afternoon." Jim gave a nod in Lucky's direction. The man's nickname was appropriate as always—lucky son of a bitch, getting everything his heart desired. At least he had a good heart—big and warm and not *too* full of himself. Jim managed a smile that was sincere. "Fingers crossed, man. See you guys in the morning."

This time, he led Thomas out of the room on his goddamn aching knees.

CHAPTER SEVEN

As Jim had known, Ashley wasn't at all dismayed that the schedule had changed and they were starting the morning at the physically punishing O-course.

He was dismayed enough for both of them as he forced himself not to limp through the breakfast line. He helped himself to a small mountain of scrambled eggs, a pile of toast, and two mugs of coffee.

Jesus, he was tired. His knees had kept him up most of the night—icing hadn't helped and he'd refused to take the painkiller the captain had prescribed. There just weren't enough hours left when he'd finally gone to bed—if he'd taken it, he'd still be feeling drugged this morning.

It was Jim's own fault for disregarding Dunk's suggestion that he take a scooter on last night's hike. Five miles hadn't seemed like any kind of big deal. Also, he'd wanted Ashley to be challenged by his limitations, and she wouldn't have been if he'd had the scooter.

But okay. He'd done what he'd done, and today's pain and fatigue was what it was. He didn't have to like it, he just had to do it—get through the day, that is.

Meanwhile Ashley—who'd only gotten a bit more sleep than he had—was sitting alone at a table, eating her breakfast while reading through her Team Leader packet. She was studying it with far more focus and care than it deserved.

Jim wasn't surprised. The woman was a direction-reader, which admittedly was a useful skill. He'd noted that last night when, even despite the flashlight's dim glow, she'd read the application instructions on the bug repellent wipes. Some people—and yeah, he tended to lean toward that particular subset—preferred to figure things out on the fly. Dive in headfirst, and if SNAFUs happened, only *then* read the directions.

Which could be dangerous. It went against the age-old SEAL adage, *Never assume.*

But in the case of the Team Leader packet—Jim had glanced through it last night while he was not-sleeping—there really wasn't all that much to learn.

In some ways it was standard officer bullshit. But unlike a Naval officer, SEAL World TLs didn't have any real command status. The job was more that of a liaison to Jim, to Dunk, and to the hospital corpsman. Because of that, Ashley had to carry a bag with a phone, a walkie-talkie in case cell service failed, and a rudimentary med kit.

Exactly what she didn't need—a few extra pounds of gear to weigh her down.

"You can delegate," Jim said in lieu of a greeting as he set his tray onto her table, and awkwardly lifted his legs over the bench so that he could sit opposite her. Ow, and *ow*. "Assign a team member, or even me, to carry the team's bag."

Ashley looked up and managed a smile. "Good morning."

Jesus, angels sang because that smile was pure blinding sunshine. He had to look away, ungracefully digging into his eggs. "Well, it's morning, that's true."

"Your knees survive the hike?" she leaned forward slightly and lowered her voice to ask.

"I'm fine." *Shit.* Now that he'd pictured that stupid word-cloud, he was going to see it every time that idiocy came out of his mouth.

Ashley wasn't fooled—he could see disbelief swimming in her observant gray eyes. But she co-signed his BS. "That's great," she said. "Because I can't *wait* to be dragged up and over that six foot wall by Bull and Todd. And FYI, I cannot hand off the Team Leader's bag." She pointed down to one of the pages in front of her. "Says so right here."

Ah, damnit, really...? "We could pretend we didn't read that," Jim countered.

"Too late," she told him. "I won't lie. Besides, if I'm doing this, I'm *doing* this."

She was dead serious, and Jim found himself not just respecting her, but really liking her. Her resourcefulness last night hadn't been just a fluke, and her sense of humor was solid. She was as shiny and gleaming and beautiful inside as she was out, and he found himself thinking about last night, when she'd handed him back his shirt, as she stood bedraggled and still drenched, her clothes glued to her lithe body, her shirt rendered transparent. She was not well-endowed up top, but her nipples were enticingly dark, and those long, strong, shapely, smooth legs that he'd seen when she'd worn running shorts would more than make up for her lack of breast size when she wrapped them around him and—

What.

The hell?

What was wrong with him? He found himself liking her because she was smart and funny and honorable, so his immediate response was to picture her naked and think about what it would be like to screw her...?

Now her words from the other night echoed in his head: *You're a part of the problem.*

At the time, he'd thought she was being overly dramatic, but damn it, maybe he *was* if he couldn't sit here and have a simple conversation with an attractive woman without getting a hard-on.

This was why there weren't women in the teams—except, nope. That kind of thinking was first cousin to victim-blaming—of putting the responsibility for safety against crimes like sexual assault purely on the backs of women, because "men couldn't help themselves." Which was damned insulting to men—implying that they were weak, lacking in control, and morally incapable of keeping their pants zipped.

"Jesus," he muttered.

Now Ashley was looking at him quizzically, so he focused on their conversation. What had they been discussing? His gaze fell on the team leader packet on the table in front of her. Right. The requirement for her to always carry the team's communication and medical bag.

"Maybe it's negotiable," he suggested. "Carrying the bag. How important can it be? I didn't even notice it when I read through the packet."

"This type of fine print is called *boilerplate*," she told him. "That generally means non-negotiable."

"Come on," he said. "You're a lawyer. *Everything's* negotiable."

"I wish," she said, looking down again at the document on the table in front of her. She sighed. "Oh, God, I *do* really wish..." But instead of finishing her thought, she shook her head and forced a smile.

"What?" Jim asked around a bite of toast. "Maybe I can be your fairy godmother, you know, make your wish come true."

She laughed at that, but shook her head again. "I wish I was really in charge of the team—that *team leader* really meant team *leader*. So, unless you can re-write these rules…"

He shrugged expansively. "Navy SEAL."

She laughed again, but this time rolled her eyes. "You say that a lot—as if it's your catch-phrase, or… It means whatever you need it to mean in the moment, doesn't it?"

She was right about that. "In this case," he told her, "it means that rewriting the rules is kinda our jam."

"With all due respect, sir, please don't say *jam*."

They both looked up to see Thomas King carrying his tray toward the bussing area.

"Too old?" Jim asked the younger man with a laugh.

"And too not-from-California," Thomas grinned back at him. "Please also purge *cowabunga* from your vocabulary, sir. And, Dunk asked me to tell you that he's finally got a few minutes to spare," the young SEAL continued. He gave both a nod and a *Ma'am* to Ashley as he then continued on his way.

Jim finished up his eggs with one last large forkful. "Gotta run," he told Ashley as he stood up. Ow and ow. "Meet you out at the O. Don't forget—this morning's exercise is a *team* event."

"Believe me, I'm well aware of that." She nodded as he took his tray toward the corner with the trash cans and dirty dish basins.

But was she? Really…? As Jim glanced back at Ashley, she gave him one last rueful smile.

"Think about it—*team*," he told her, but he was far enough away now that the noise of the clattering dishes made it impossible for her to hear him, and as he watched, she shook her head, frowning slightly to signal that she wasn't able to read his lips. So he tapped his head instead, but he could see that she still didn't understand, so he held up six fingers, but she still shook her head.

Sadly, he couldn't be any less cryptic. His team leader had to figure it out for herself—best he could do was make broad hints.

As he went to talk to Dunk—about Ashley, although his conversational subtopic of how best to help her was now on hold as a discussion of team leader duties took priority—her words echoed in his head. *I can't wait to be dragged up and over that wall by Bull and Todd.*

Yeah, that was gonna be hard to watch.

He was certain that Ashley would figure it out eventually. He just hoped—for his sake as well as her own—that it would be sooner rather than later.

Bull "helped" Ashley up to the top of the O-course wall—one hand on her butt, the other beneath her arm, which ended up, yes, on her breast.

It could've been accidental—yeah, right, in some alternate universe.

He somewhat laboriously pulled himself up and slid down the other side as she got her bearings and teetered there, balancing on the top. She risked a glance over at Jim, who was leaning against the fence across the compound. He'd absolutely seen that—his eyes were narrowed and his mouth tight. But he didn't stop them—he just went back to looking down at his phone.

"Come on, move it!" Bull shouted up at her, once he was securely on the ground, with a gesture that was half impatience and half *I'll catch you.*

"No, I got it," she said, because the wall wasn't *that* high, and sliding down was much easier than clambering up—although in truth, she'd really only needed a clasped-handed toe boost from him, which of course wouldn't have allowed him to grope her as thoroughly. "Back off, Mr. Edison, give me space."

Of course, he didn't. He moved closer, hands outstretched as she slid down—right into a crotch grab, God *damn* it.

"I got it, move back!" she said, louder this time as she twisted to get away from his hands and his leering, laughing face. There was enough of an edge to her voice that Jim looked up again from whatever he was doing—sending texts or emails, or God, maybe even live-tweeting this debacle—during this so-called *planning phase* of their first morning exercise.

Before Team One was officially timed as they ran the obstacle course, their task was to figure out the best way to get through it as quickly as possible, considering their individual limitations—i.e. *her* limitations.

Bull just laughed at Ashley's raised voice, so Todd laughed, too, as Clark and Kenneth hovered anxiously nearby, and that was it. Something in her snapped.

"Okay!" she clapped her hands together. "That's it. We're good. I got it—I know how we're doing this." She forced herself to sound cheerful, rather than enraged—because enraged *never* worked with men like Bull and Todd.

Jim headed toward them, his phone finally back in his pocket, his face and eyes lit with interest as he looked from Ashley to Bull and back.

"*You* got it?" Bull asked, belligerence in his voice. "Yeah, sorry, it's not up to *you*. Todd and I have the most experience."

"What's your strategy?" Jim asked.

Bull turned to look at the SEAL. "Move as fast as we can while we drag the chick and the hipsters over the fuh—"

Jim spoke loudly over him. "Team Leader, what's your strategy?" He was looking at her, because, yes, *she* was the TL.

Bull protested. "Brah, the team-leader thing is only an honorary title—"

Jim glared at Bull with ice in his eyes. "It's *Lieutenant* or *LT* or *Sir* when you address me, and *Team Leader DeWitt* or *TL* or *Ma'am* when you address your team leader."

"No, I mean, *yes*, LT—" Bull, of course, chose the least formal way of addressing the SEAL instructor "—but you're new so, you probably don't realize that the TL is random, you know, just someone with administrative skills to act as a go-between for the team and the camp."

"Incorrect, Mr. Edison," Jim shot back. "Your SEAL instructor, which last time I checked was *me*, has the discretion to decide specifically what the team leader's duties will entail. I could see how you might've missed it. It's in the fine print in the TL's packet."

Ashley sighed and shook her head, because that wasn't even close to true, but then Jim turned to aim his next words at her.

"You'll be getting a revised team leader packet," he informed her, "with that change included." He pulled out his phone and held it up as if *Exhibit A*. "I just wrote it and got Dunk to sign off on it," he added. "So please do tell us, TL, what is *your* strategy for the O-course."

This time Bull and Todd remained silent—they both respected his status as a SEAL officer, and took the military-like structure of the team seriously. But the look in their eyes said *You don't seriously expect* her *to have a* real *strategy,* and *We wouldn't need a strategy if we weren't on a team with a bunch of losers.*

Ashley worked to make her voice sound even. Pleasant. Not as if she'd just fended off a sexual assault from an idiot. "Let Bull and Todd go first, so we're not in their way, while Kenneth, Clark, and I help each other."

Bull and Todd immediately started making noise about that, but Jim held up one hand, and somewhat miraculously, they shut up.

"That's smart," Jim said. "Pairing Bull and Todd up—letting the team members otherwise get out of each others' way. Five—or *six*—people going over an obstacle like the wall or the cargo net at the exact same time isn't easy or even possible, at least not on this smaller course."

He widened his eyes at her, and in a sudden flash, she realized that she'd completely forgotten about the fact that because they were a team of five, they were allowed to ask their instructor to participate in team events. Which this was. Completely. Which made them a team of six, which meant...

Suddenly, she remembered him holding up six fingers, in that silent message he'd tried sending her across the mess hall. Dear God, she was so tired, she wasn't thinking clearly...

"Bull's with Todd, and Kenneth's with Clark," Jim prompted her now, "leaving..."

"You with me," she finished. Thank God. Oh, please, God, don't let Jim be a groper, too. But then she realized this team configuration only worked in theory. "What about your knees?"

"What about 'em?"

"Can you even... I mean... I don't want you to..."

"Hell, yeah. On *this* course...? I'll be fine." He winced. "I know I say that a lot, but really. I got this, TL."

Ashley gazed into his blue eyes. *Please, don't be lying about your knees, and please, for the love of all that is holy, don't also be a douchebag and use this as an excuse to put your hands all over me...*

He smiled wryly, almost as if he'd read her mind. And after glancing over at Bull, who'd moved off a bit to mutter privately to Todd, he lowered his voice to say, "I thought you were finally gonna..." He shook his head almost regretfully, and repeated what he'd told her before. "It's okay to get angry," but then added, "I promise I won't let you kill him."

She laughed her surprise at that. "Then, it doesn't matter, because without killing him, nothing would change."

"Hmmm. You actually believe that, don't you?"

"I believe it, because it's true," she told him.

Jim nodded. "It's not, because it's not only about him—you're part of this, too, but okay. We don't have time to discuss that now, because we're waiting on your command."

Her *command*. She liked that word. It was strong and decisive, instead of wimpy and uncertain. She straightened her shoulders and raised her voice in a team-leaderly manner. "Let's do it, then," she commanded. "Let's go."

CHAPTER EIGHT

God *damn* it.

Jim sat in the shade under his RV's awning, knowing that he should go inside and ice his knees.

"You okay?"

Ashley. She was heading to her trailer after having lunch in the mess—Team One had another hour of down time before they were scheduled up at the paintball field. She was still dressed in the cargo shorts and sweat-stained T-shirt she'd worn throughout the morning's strenuous exercises—Red Sox cap on her head. She had to be tired, too, but she was hiding it well.

Jim thought about lying. He was fine, *fine, fine-fine-fine...* But he suddenly heard an echo of his own voice, earlier, right after Bull had groped her—telling Ashley that it was okay to get angry. And maybe—just maybe—it was *also* okay for Jim himself to be honest about what *he* was going through.

So he tried it out. The N-sound was hard to make, but he pushed and it came out, "Nnnn…" He couldn't quite make it a full *no*. But from the deepening look of concern on her face, he knew he'd gotten the point across.

She came closer. "How can I help?"

"You could knit me a new career."

She laughed—just a little—as she also frowned. "Who told you I knit? Clark." She shook her head as she dumped her team-leader bag on the ground next to the table. "Did he mention I was sixteen when I last attempted a sweater, no probably not. Do I need to find Lieutenant King or is there ice inside?" She pointed to his RV door, and he managed a nod.

"Yeah, there's ice, but it's a mess in there…"

"Since I'm pretty sure any ice will be in the freezer, that's a non-issue," she shot back as she opened the screen and went inside. "God, I *knew* you were hurt—it happened right after the cargo net, didn't it? You twisted your knee in the sand."

Yes, but he rather desperately didn't want to talk about it. Then he didn't have to, as she changed the subject. Her voice carried clearly from the trailer's open windows.

"You know, you would make a great lawyer."

Jim laughed. A few years back, he'd briefly toyed with the idea, although most of the SEALs he knew had laughed their asses off. It had turned into a joke that was nearly as long-lived as his nickname: Spaceman Slade as a Perry Mason-esque lawyer, punching opposing counsel in the face, then turning to the bench to say, *Your Honor, the defense rests.* "Yeah, I don't think so."

Ashley came out his RV with the ziplock baggies of fresh ice that Thomas had dropped off that morning, and the hand towels Jim had hung on the freezer door handle to protect his skin from the biting cold.

"Why not?" she asked. "I think you'd be really good at it. That codicil to the team leader agreement... You wrote it perfectly."

"Codicil," he repeated with a laugh as he took the frozen packets and the towels from her. He layered them onto both of his knees—as if that was actually going to help. "I didn't know it was a codicil, it was just... me getting what I wanted."

"No," she said, sitting down in the other chair and settling in, as if she planned to stay for a while, "it was you getting what *I* wanted. Which is exactly what lawyers do for their clients."

She was serious, and Jim laughed again. "Going to law school would be... a rather huge challenge."

Ashley shrugged. "Navy SEAL. Isn't that what you always say?"

"Well, yeah," Jim said, "but... also Navy SEAL...? Law school is, like, two solid years of sitting still."

"Three," she corrected him.

"Oh, even better."

"Except maybe if you sit still—still-*ish*—for three years," she pointed out, "your knees might actually heal."

"Not enough," he said grimly.

"Enough to be a lawyer," she said. "Oh my God! I just realized—you could join JAG."

JAG stood for Judge Advocate General—the legal arm of the Navy. "It's not some club with an on-line signup," he countered. "You don't just *join* JAG."

The look she shot him was one of amusement. "You know what I mean. JAG needs good lawyers—I happen to know they're actively recruiting. And you can't seriously think that the Navy wouldn't do everything humanly possible to *keep* you—a SEAL officer? I mean, assuming you want to stay in. Although, you'd definitely earn more money if you left and went into the public sector. *Way* more. There's no law firm on the planet who wouldn't salivate at the idea of including a Navy SEAL lawyer on their website's short list of associates, so... The big question is: *Do* you want to stay in...?"

It was a little surreal, sitting here, actually talking about this. If she'd asked, *Do you want to stay in the Navy as a SEAL,* he'd respond without hesitation. That question was as absurd as *Do you want to continue breathing?* Absolutely, yes.

But that's not what she'd asked. There was a silent part to her question which was *If you can't continue to do the very hands-on, physically grueling work of a SEAL...*

Jim went with the truth. "I don't know. As anything besides a SEAL...? Sitting behind a desk...?" He shook his head in frustration and tried to move the focus off of himself. "How do you know so much about JAG anyway?"

"There's a military recruiting office in the strip mall where I work," she told him. "I've had lunch a few times with one of the chiefs."

"Oh," he said as he realized of *course* she was dating some-one—how could this woman *not* be dating someone? She was beautiful and smart and funny and kind...

"Also," she continued with a slightly mischievous smile that lit her up completely, "when I was a kid, I watched a TV show about a JAG lawyer. Lawyer shows tend to be hyper-fictional—the law is actually brain-numbingly slow-moving, so shows about lawyers aren't exactly reality based. Even courtroom *action*—" she made air quotes "—is deadly slow. But this show had lots of eye candy that was perfect for a twelve-year-old. Those white uniforms..."

"My closet is filled with them." And *that* came out sounding weirdly flirtatious, which wasn't his intention. Although at the news that she was dating someone, he'd immediately flashed back to the late morning, when they'd paired up to go through the O-course.

Unlike Bull, Jim had been careful about where he'd put his hands on Ashley, working hard to make sure his touch was both respectful and impersonal. But there had been a moment that had rattled him and stuck now in his memory—in fact, it was playing on repeat—as he'd helped her over the cargo net. They'd made the climb easily, with him cradling her entire body—his arms around her, her back against his front. She was essentially sitting on his lap as they ascended the netting together, his mouth just beside her ear as he'd instructed her how to move with him—to keep the ropes taut and stable.

As businesslike as he'd tried to be, he hadn't been able to keep from noting how perfectly she fit against him, and how freaking good it felt to hold her close like that.

And how crazy-good she smelled...

Then, just suddenly, like *bang*, as they'd reached the top and maneuvered their way to the other side, every time he touched her it seemed to burn his hands, and on their way back down he was hyper-aware of all of the places they were skin-to-skin—her arms against his, the calves of their legs... And right before they hit the sand, she turned her head and his face and lips were pressed against the softness of her neck, where he actually tasted the salt of her sweat, and his head had damn near exploded.

And he stupidly—*stupidly*—landed wrong in his haste to not, like, lick her or nuzzle more deeply into her neck or do something equally and insanely inappropriate. And because of that, he'd twisted the crap out of his knee.

Jesus, he was an idiot.

Jim now cleared his throat and attempted to explain. "If I stayed in, went the JAG route, at least I wouldn't have to buy a bunch of new suits." Okay, now he just sounded stupid. But that was fine, because he clearly *was* stupid. Stupid to twist his knee, and stupid to think that she wasn't dating someone—a chief in the Navy, to boot.

Freaking chiefs ran the Navy—capable and down-to-earth, reliable and steady...

But Ashley was nodding as if his weird mention of the dress unis that filled his closet actually made sense. "Sometimes when I can't decide what to do," she told him, "I make a list of all the little things that come to mind—both pro and con. I mean, it's pretty clear you want to stay in, but as a SEAL. And yeah, you won't have to buy a new wardrobe if you go the JAG route, but... Will putting on your uniform every day smack you in the face with a reminder of what you can't be anymore...? How are you going to *feel*?"

Oh, Jesus. Seriously...?

She kept going. "But on the other hand, you've been in the

Navy for years and you know how the military system works, it's familiar. Corporate America is very different—you'll be tossed in with much younger people who've been playing the corporate game since college—possibly even earlier. How's *that* going to feel—like you're in uncharted territory, uncertain and off-balance, or... maybe that actually appeals to you. Maybe it'll feel like an exciting new adventure."

Jim nodded, because she seemed to be waiting for some kind of response. But all this talk about second guessing how he was going to *feel*...? Nope. He couldn't even put a name to whatever this shittiness was that he was feeling right now, let alone guess how shitty he was going to *feel* in the future. To hell with that—shitty or extra-desperately-shitty—he had to box it all up and just get through the day, the way he'd always done.

But a pro and con list...? *That* was a useful decision-making tool. So, pro: he already had the uniforms and he hated shopping for clothes. Con: dress whites were a freaking pain in his ass—trying to stay clean while wearing white was a challenge for the most fastidious Naval officer, and he was far from that. Although, he only had to wear the whites half of the year, unless he was stationed somewhere tropical, like Hawaii.

Pro: He might be stationed in Hawaii. He liked Hawaii.

Pro: Even though he was no longer officially a SEAL, he'd continue to wear his Budweiser on his uni day in and day out—and damned if that didn't mean something to him. Huh. In fact, it meant a lot.

But three years of law school... Big, *big* con. Jim looked over to find Ashley just quietly watching him, as if she knew he was constructing that list in his head and didn't want to interrupt.

"Tell me about law school," he asked.

"It's hard," she said. "It's deadly dull. But the work is the work—you put your head down and get it done. You'll have to learn to read more slowly... But I did it, so I know that you can, too. You're already incredibly patient—you proved that today, on the O-course. You just have to learn to be patient with yourself. If you decide to go—wherever you end up—I would highly recommend talking to other students and digging a bit and getting a list of the best professors and teachers. A good instructor can be life or death in some of the required classes." But then she laughed at herself. "Not *really* life or death, like it is for a Navy SEAL. But try staying awake in Tort Reform with a teacher who doesn't at least attempt to make it entertaining..."

He nodded. "Where'd you go?"

"Northeastern, in Boston," she said. "Far enough from New York, but not too far."

"Not Harvard?" he asked.

She laughed. "No, thanks. I didn't even apply. My father was... less than pleased about *that*. But Northeastern's got some great social justice programs. And since that's the direction I wanted to go from the start..."

Jim nodded. "Best part of being a lawyer...?"

Ashley thought about that for a moment. "I get to help people," she finally said. "Particularly women and children, who don't have a lot of power."

"Worst part?"

She smiled. "That's easy. Dealing with other lawyers." She corrected herself. "Some other lawyers." But then changed it again, "Most. Big overlap in the Venn diagram of lawyers and a-holes."

"So now I know," Jim teased her, "why you were so quick to jump on the idea that I'd make a *great* lawyer." He made air quotes around the word.

"No!" she said, laughing. "Oh, my God, no!"

"Um-hmm," he said, smiling back at her, because she was just too freaking adorable—she was even blushing a little as she realized she'd walked right into that one. And all of a sudden, their gazes locked and something clicked and created a burst of sudden heat, and he had to quickly look away, because that was not okay. He cleared his throat. "So, um... Tell me about your chief. Is he temporary or FTS—full-time support? How long's he been in the Reserves?"

Ashley was clearly confused. "I'm sorry... I... My what?"

"You just told me you're dating a chief—the recruiter...?"

She laughed in surprise. "No, I said I had *lunch* with... Chief Gordon. *Kathleen* Gordon. Not a date—she's very happily married. And she's temporary—relatively new to the reserves." She shook her head in combined amusement and disgust.

"Damnit," Jim said, "I've gone and failed your feminist test. Again."

"No," she said. "*Now* you've failed my feminist test by assuming I *have* a feminist test for you to fail, instead of simply apologizing and promising you'll try harder to live more fully in a world where a chief from a military recruiting office might be a woman. Kathy's really good at her job, by the way."

Touché. Jim nodded. "Forgive me, twice, because I also absolutely misspoke. What I meant to say is that I've failed *my* feminist test. I blast through life, assuming I'm an ally—that I'm one of the good ones, the *safe* ones, someone give me a cookie for being so freaking wonderful—and then I do this, and trip over my dick."

Ashley laughed. "At least you recognize that as a negative. Some men just, like, noisily windmill all over the place, completely oblivious to the fact that they—and everyone else trapped in the room, God help them—are tripping over their dicks."

Jim laughed, too, although his laughter was mixed with a soupçon of shock and surprise—*happy* surprise. Windmill—which meant waving one's penis in a circle—was a word he absolutely didn't expect to use in a conversation with Ashley DeWitt. On the other hand, he'd learned last night that she *was* intriguingly funny. "I wasn't aware there was noise involved in windmilling. Unless the dicks in question are so giant and moving so fast they break the sound barrier...?"

She laughed even harder at that. "Giant's not usually the case," she said, grinning back at him. "In fact, it's usually the opposite of giant. And it's noisy because there's accompanied screaming or grunting or... maybe even manly burping and farting."

And now she'd said *fart*. It was possible he'd just fallen in love. "You apparently know men quite well."

"Sadly, I do," she said.

And now, as they smiled into each other eyes, when that flare of heated awareness arose, Jim didn't look away. Although... "How do you not have a boyfriend?" he asked, but then adjusted. "Or maybe a... *girl*friend...?"

Ashley's smile deepened at that. "Boyfriend," she said. "And I don't have one because I have a terrible ex-fiancé."

"Ouch," he said. "How terrible?"

"On a scale from one to ten...?" she said. "A solid twelve."

"Well... congratulations on not marrying him," Jim told her. "Some people don't find out they've got someone with a twelve on the terribleness scale until *after* the vows, and that's gotta suck even worse, so... Good job. Go, you."

She laughed a little at that, but the expression on her face was pensive. "I never really thought of it that way, but you're right. Go, me."

"I'm not up on my terribleness-scale ratings, is a twelve a... cheater?"

"No, no," she said. "Cheating's a ten."

"So... serial killer, then. Man, I hate when that happens. You meet someone, and everything's going really well, but then they're all *I must now show you my collection of ears.*"

Ashley laughed at that as he'd hoped she would, because damn, when she laughed something warm shifted in his chest and made the day bearable. More than bearable—it actually made it pleasant. What was happening...?

"I'm pretty sure Brad isn't a serial killer," she told him, "but after we broke up, well, he had trouble learning that *no* meant *no*, and *over* meant *over*. That's one of the reasons why I'm here, because now, suddenly, he's back."

"Back?" Jim said. "As in *back*? As in, you currently have an active stalker and you didn't think that might be something you'd want to mention...? Jesus, Ash, we've gotta work some hand-to-hand self-defense into your schedule, and I know you're not a fan of firearms and I agree completely that getting a weapon without having either the training or impetus to use it properly would be a big mistake, but we can certainly take pictures that you can post on social media—like, *Look, here I am getting some serious weapons training at SEAL World dot dot dot—*"

She interrupted him. "Thank you, but no, because Brad's really not dangerous."

"Sorry, but I disagree. A grown man who hasn't yet mastered *no means no...*?"

"He's been... led to believe that when *I* say *no* I don't mean *no*." She shook her head. "I don't think he holds that belief universally."

"So it's just *you* he treats like shit."

She winced. "Yes, but no. It's really just more of an... inconvenience and... it creates a little... discomfort."

Jim looked at her sitting there across from him. Even dressed way down in her camp clothes, with her hair sweaty and a streak of dirt on her chin, she was breathtakingly beautiful. Her sense of humor was crazy. She was highly intelligent—but someone had messed with her, badly, even back before the stalker ex-fiancé had made the scene.

"What does it take to get you angry?" he asked her. "Like, drop-dead seething, spitting-out-shards-of-your-teeth angry?"

Ashley looked surprised, and for a moment she seemed to seriously consider his question, but when she spoke, she neatly sidestepped it. "Getting angry solves nothing."

"Okay," he said. "Great. But if you *were* gonna get angry, say, if God suddenly came down from heaven and she's all *Ashley DeWitt, if you let yourself get angry, I won't let one single child go to sleep hungry tonight.* What has to happen to push you to that veins-popping-out-on-your-forehead place?"

She took a deep breath—and his freaking phone rang.

His instinct was to immediately silence it, but it was lying out on the table between them, and Dunk's name appeared clearly on the screen. And because they'd spent the morning working closely together as team leader and team instructor, she knew that he'd been hoping to get Dunk's ear again today, even for just ten minutes.

She didn't know that the topic of conversation was going to be *her.*

And maybe it was because his question had spooked her, but she was already up on her feet and grabbing her TL bag as she said, "You should take that. I need to make a pit-stop in my trailer before this afternoon, anyway, change into jeans and…"

And just like that, she was gone.

"Yo," Jim answered Dunk's call.

"I got about twenty," Dunk said without ceremony. "You to me, or me to you?"

"Me to you, Senior," Jim said as he took the ice off his aching knees. "I'll be right there."

"Coffee?"

"Please." Sweet Jesus. Not only was Dunk's office halfway to the paintball field, Jim wanted this conversation to happen behind a door that tightly closed.

And the fact that there was a coffeemaker in Dunk's office sure as hell didn't hurt.

CHAPTER NINE

Ashley arrived a few minutes early at the double-wide trailer designated as one of the official paintball safety zones. It was a repurposed construction-site trailer, with a wooden ramp leading up to the door.

The building was dark, but she tried the knob anyway. The door was tightly locked, which confirmed that she'd gotten here before Jim.

The trailer sat along the fence line of the paintball grounds—a large, secluded area of woods. The only way into and out of the fenced grounds was via this trailer. Although there *was* another designated safety zone in a smaller trailer that was parked up at the north end of the expansive grounds. It not only provided a second safe place to de-mask, but it also contained a medical kit and a supply of water.

This was only day two of the week, and she'd already heard "masks stay on out on the paintball grounds, no exceptions" many dozens of times. She suspected, during this afternoon's paintball equipment training session, that she was going to hear it many times more.

"I'm all right. Just stop."

"Well, you don't *look* all right."

Ashley turned to see Clark and Kenneth coming down the trail, bickering.

"I'll be okay," Kenneth insisted. He saw that Ashley had heard them, and gave her a smile that was meant to be reassuring, but Clark was right. Kenneth looked pale—paler than normal—and his smile was forced. "Lunch didn't agree with me. It's really no big deal."

"Lunch," Clark said, "*and* breakfast, *and* dinner last night, *and* lunch and dinner the night before…"

"You both eat way too fast," Ashley pointed out.

"It's been going on for a while," Clark told her. "The stomach aches. It's been weeks, actually. It gets a little better, but then it gets worse. And each time it gets worse it's *worse*."

Kenneth shook his head. "That's just not true."

"Yes, it is."

"And you're not just eating too much crap?" Ashley asked. Their diets were atrocious at school—candy and soda and pizza and cheese-steaks and sugared breakfast cereals, washed down with beer and stout and Jell-O shots. Of course, here at camp, they weren't drinking since they were both underage, and the junk food wasn't as plentiful, although she suspected that one of their giant suitcases had been entirely filled with snacks.

"He's barely eating anything at all," Clark reported.

"That's not good." Ashley pulled both boys aside, lowering her voice as Bull and Todd arrived. Now they were only waiting for Jim—Lieutenant Slade. "You think I should call Lieutenant King?"

"No," Kenneth said, as Clark said, "Yes!"

Kenneth turned to give Clark a withering look, that—along with his clipped British delivery—called to mind the Dowager Countess from *Downton Abbey*. "To do what…? Rub my tum-tum…?"

"No, to just make sure you're really okay," Clark argued.

"Lieutenant King's a medic—a first responder—not a doctor," Kenneth pointed out. "Am I bleeding? No. Am I on fire? Not since the last time I checked. He'll take my blood pressure, which I'm sure is dead normal, and suggest I take the afternoon off, feet up in the trailer, to which I say, *No, thank you.* Paintball's the one activity I actually *want* to learn, and, if you must know the truth, I suspect my problem is that I'm celiac." He turned to Ashley. "Louise was having similar symptoms and has just been diagnosed."

"Who's Louise?" she asked.

"My twin," Kenneth reported.

Kenneth had a twin. Wow.

"Oh, my God, of course you're celiac if Louise is," Clark realized, "I mean, you're identical twins."

"Not identical," Ashley pointed out.

"I've seen her picture," Clark insisted. "They look exactly alike."

"Because we're *siblings*," Kenneth hissed. "We not *exactly* identical. Do the math, Clark."

Ashley did it for him. "Male, female…?"

"*Oh!*" he said. "Yeah. Right. Huh." But then he also realized, "When was Louise diagnosed, and how come you didn't tell me?"

"I got an email from her about a week ago," Kenneth said. "I was sort of still processing it."

"Celiac," Clark said. "That *sucks.*"

"Since we're twins, we share a lot of DNA," Kenneth said, "but that doesn't necessarily mean I have it. It is, however, more likely, and since I haven't been feeling well..."

"Celiac," Clark said. "Oh, man, no more pasta...? I don't think I could live without pasta."

"It's not life-threatening," Kenneth told Ashley. "Certainly not at this stage. I just feel a bit under the weather. Some moments are a little bit worse, but, really..."

"No more Twinkies," Clark said.

"I'm going to mention it to both Lieutenants Slade and King," Ashley told him. "And the first thing I know they'll both ask me is if you're drinking enough water."

"I am," he told her.

"Oh, dear God," Clark said, "no more *beer*...?"

Ashley looked at her brother. "How is that helping?"

"No more Italian bread," Clark lamented, "or croissants, bagels, pizza, *donuts*..."

"Why didn't I tell you, you asked," Kenneth said. "Hello. *This* is why."

It was then that Jim appeared. He was driving one of Dunk's golf buggies and as he pulled up by the paintball field fence, he looked from Ashley—standing with Kenneth and Clark—to Bull and Todd.

"Sorry, I'm late," he said as he cut the electric motor. "My meeting with Senior Chief Duncan ran a little long."

"You're actually right on time," Ashley informed him as he climbed out of the cart. He managed not to wince, but she didn't miss the muscle flexing in his jaw as he clenched his teeth against what must've been pain from his knees.

Still he managed to sound breezy. "Early is on-time in SEAL World," he reminded them as he moved toward the back of the cart. "And on-time is late. So first round's on me in the lounge tonight."

No one responded—team spirit was definitely suppressed—so Ashley spoke up. "You really don't have to—"

Jim must've realized that almost half of the team couldn't drink, so he quickly amended with, "Or the equivalent in video game plays."

And although Clark quietly *all-right*ed, Kenneth's smile was wan. It was clear that Jim noticed, because he glanced at Ashley again, a question in his sharp blue eyes as he reached for the huge trunk—some kind of storage container made of heavy duty black plastic—that was in the back of the cart.

"Hold up, LT!" No way was she letting him carry that. God, his knees... "Clark and... um, Todd, please," Ashley called in her best Team Leader's voice. "Get that trunk. Lieutenant, if you don't mind, Kenneth needs to speak to you for a sec."

If Jim was surprised by her commanding tone, he didn't show it. He simply stepped back as Clark scrambled over to get one end of the trunk. Todd took a little bit longer to snap to, so Jim handed the key to the trailer—old school, on a ring—to Clark. "You'll need the keypad code, too," he told her brother, leaning in to share the code in a lower voice that Ashley couldn't hear. And then, no doubt because Clark had reached him first, he drove home the point that the kid was in charge of *Operation: Move the Trunk* by ordering Todd, "Help Clark move it all the way onto the field." Back to Clark, "Find us a good patch of shade. We'll be talking safety, and that's gonna take a while." And with that, he turned toward Kenneth.

Which left Ashley with Bull.

"Safety instructions take longer when half the team are morons," the big man informed her with a smugness to his tone.

Don't worry. We don't mind going slowly so that you and Todd can keep up. Things she'd never dare to say aloud, because frankly, escalating the hostility never worked. Not only was it rude, it was ineffective. Getting angry didn't help, either—all it did was make her feel more powerless and impotent, as well as potentially putting her into danger.

Although the sad truth was, Ashley had spent most of her life feeling powerless, impotent, and in danger. *But at least no one could ever call her impolite.*

That wayward thought reverberated in her head as she gazed into Bull's mocking eyes, and all she could think was of all the ways he'd been *unbelievably* rude to her over the past few days.

He was an a-hole—no question.

But what was *she*...? She'd earned her "Politeness" Girl Scout Badge a gazillion times over, and... She had exactly nothing to show for it—aside from the giant boot treadmarks on her doormatof-a-face.

"Hey, TL." Jim's voice interrupted her and she looked over to where he was standing with Kenneth, near the golf-cart-dune-buggy hybrid.

"I'm good with Kenneth staying in the program, if you are," Jim told her. "He says he's hydrating sufficiently. I'll inform the kitchen, and we'll make sure he's got gluten-free options for each meal."

"You really can do that?" Ashley asked.

Jim's smile was infectious. "Navy SEAL," he reminded her. "Come on, let's get in there. We got about five thousand safety rules to cover before we get to the fun part."

"The fun part…?" she echoed as she followed them into the trailer, and then almost immediately out the other side into an expansive fenced-in area filled with trees and other obstacles.

"The fun part *isn't* getting hit with one of these pellets," Jim told his team, after distributing both the masks and the air-guns that were called *markers* because they fired pellets of paint that exploded on contact and marked their targets.

He'd lectured, in some detail, about the tanks of compressed air, as well as the hoppers that fed the marble-sized paintball pellets into the markers. And although both the tanks and hoppers had yet to be dispersed, he'd passed around a handful of the pellets, which were a non-toxic, biodegradable mix of oil, gelatin, and water-soluble dye.

"It stings," he told them. "The pellets come at you, somewhere between one-sixty and one-ninety miles per hour, so yeah. It stings. Gentlemen, wear your athletic cups. But when it comes to velocity, combined with the three meter rule—which is…?"

"No firing at anyone closer than three meters," his team all repeated, in unison, although Bull and Todd mumbled unenthusiastically. They'd been through this before and were making sure that Jim knew they were bored.

Tough shit.

Jim hammered it home. "And in American, rounding up, three meters is…?"

"Ten feet," they all said.

"Good. But you combine the three-meter rule with the relatively low velocity of the paintball pellets," he said, "and you get an astonishingly high rate of bouncers—pellets that bounce off without breaking. And what's the rule, Team Leader, when a pellet bounces off of you without breaking?"

"Keep going," Ashley said. "You're not dead."

"And what's the consensus on wipers?" Jim asked. "Mr. DeWitt?"

"No one likes wipers," Clark said as, interestingly, neither Bull nor Todd managed to hold Jim's gaze.

Wipers were the guys—people—who, in the course of a paintball game, attempted to cheat by wiping off the paint that marked them as "dead."

"But hits to the head and face don't count," Jim reminded them. "So wipe away, if your mask gets splattered. Mr. Edison, our rule about blind-firing is...?"

Bull's body language was pure nonchalant scorn—he was leaning back on his elbows—and his laughter was dismissive. "Don't." He leaned over to add to Todd, in a stage whisper meant to be overheard, "Get caught."

"No blind firing," Jim said. Blind-firing was when you hunkered down behind a tree or another obstacle, lifted your marker up over your head, and fired without eyes on your potential target. Without eyes on your target, there was no way of knowing if your target was three meters—or three inches—away. Without eyes on, you ran the risk of hitting another player—possibly even one on your own team—in the head. And at close range, that could be dangerous.

Jim felt his ire rising as Bull and Todd high-fived and laughed. These assholes... How did Ashley manage to *not* go off on them...? "And you're right. Don't get caught—so don't do it, because you *will* get caught. FYI, Dunk's just seeded the playing field with an array of wireless mini-cams." That was an exaggeration of the truth—Dunk had installed cameras in only a few key locations. Still, it was obvious Bull and Todd didn't have the honor and integrity needed to follow the rules on their own merit. They needed to fear being seen. "Anyone caught blind-firing—or breaking *any* of the safety rules—will be ejected not just from the paintball game, but from the camp session. Is that clear?"

Ashley was the only one who responded with, "Sir, yes, sir!" Clark and Kenneth nodded, but Bull and Todd still snickered and rolled their eyes.

So Jim repeated. Loudly. While glaring at Bull and Todd. "Is. That. Clear?"

"Sir! Yes, sir!"

The smug smiles were gone, and the response was delivered without any eye rolls. Which meant that Bull and Todd were spared from dropping and doing a hundred pushups—for the moment.

Jim cleared his throat. "And the number one safety rule…?"

"Masks on at all times on the field," the entire team repeated.

Kenneth put his hand up, so Jim pointed at the kid.

"Aren't we on the field right now?" he asked in his crisply proper accent. "I mean, the rule is *Masks on before we step outside of the trailer*, yet here we are and our masks aren't on…?"

"Today is the sole exception," Jim told them. "Masks also fog up in high humidity, and for this session, I want you to see clearly. Especially as we move the topic of conversation from safety to physics. In fact, I need a volunteer." He didn't wait—he pointed at Ashley. "Team Leader, if you will. Mask and marker, too, please."

She sighed, but she didn't argue. She just pushed herself up off the ground, wiping the seat of her jeans as she moved toward him, carrying her gear.

She wasn't happy to be his "volunteer," but she trusted him. Jim could see it—on her face, in her approach, in the way she met his eyes.

She trusted him—and he brutally quashed any regret or remorse he might've been feeling, before it even registered. He'd made up his mind during his discussion with Dunk. Jim was here to teach—not to be Ashley's friend.

He told the rest of the team, "Before you put on your masks and do a little target practice with your markers—" he pointed to the outlined targets that had been painted onto a length of wooden stockade fencing that was positioned in the yard, some distance away "—TL and I are going to demonstrate how and why firing a paintball pellet from a marker is different from firing a real weapon up at the shooting range."

But as he curtly ordered Ashley, "Mask on," and took her marker out of her hands, she gave him a smile that made his heart break just a little.

And it was the ridiculousness of that—the idea that he felt anything at all, let alone something that could put a crack into his Teflon heart—made him more determined to do this—to get it done.

So he quickly attached the air canister to Ashley's marker, and then added a hopper filled with bright red paintball pellets. He also jammed his own mask on his head—to find that she still hadn't gotten her mask on properly.

"Hold this," he ordered her, brusquely pushing the faux-weapon at her.

She clutched it as he moved her mask into place—again, roughly at first. He'd do this to the entire team—a smack and a yank, making sure their masks were secure—each time they left the trailer and took the field.

But then, he steeled himself and let his hands linger on the warmth of Ashley's head, his fingers sliding through the silk of her hair, against the smoothness of her ears and jawline and neck. And Jesus, he hated this. What should've felt amazing—all that deceptive softness covering her runner's muscles and pure female strength—instead made his stomach clench with disgust. He hated the entire sorry-assed world—himself included.

Because he was the genius who'd come up with this plan, after that long conversation with Dunk.

"Don't get your hopes up," Dunk had warned Jim as they'd sat in his office, after Jim had told Dunk he wanted to try to push Ashley past her breaking point. "Some people just don't allow themselves to get angry. It's more than they *don't* let anger in—they actually *can't.*"

"Yeah, but I know her hot buttons," Jim pointed out.

"Oh, good," Dunk said dryly. "If you get me sued, settlement's coming out of your pay."

"She's not gonna sue," Jim said.

"She's a lawyer."

"She's not gonna—" Jim regrouped. "Senior, just cover your ass, okay? Tell me not to do this, write up a memo about our conversation—"

"Don't do this," Dunk said as he pushed himself out of his chair. "And *you* write the flipping memo—arrogant asshole officer, giving *me* paperwork…? If you really have to do this—but I'll say it again: *don't*—use my computer and printer and leave it on my desk so I can sign it." He shook his head as he left Jim in his office, but he also muttered "Good luck, goddamn quixotic idiot," as he closed the door behind him.

Writing that memo had made Jim late.

He now moved his hands down to Ashley's shoulders—she was wearing one of her tank tops over a running bra—she'd brought a long-sleeved shirt as the paintball rules instructed, but it was so freaking hot out she hadn't yet put it on. Her sun-kissed shoulders were warm and smooth beneath his hands. And it occurred to him that if, say, *Clark* had been his volunteer, he might've put his hands on the kid's shoulders in this exact same way. Why, then, was this different? Because, God, it was.

"You're good to go," he told her as she stood there, hanging onto her marker as she stared up at him through the hard plastic view shield of her mask.

And yeah. All that trust he'd seen in her body language had already transformed to surprise and confusion at his sudden handsy behavior. Not that he was being handsy like Bull or Todd. He most certainly wasn't grabbing her ass. And yet she now had an electric wariness that almost made her vibrate. But she didn't pull away. It was possible she was frozen.

All-righty then. Jim kept his hands on her shoulders as he turned her to face the fencing with the outlined targets. There were seven of them—all big, blocky, vaguely male outlines in clean, fresh black paint against the weather-silvered wood. "Aim for the one in the middle, TL."

As he'd expected her to do, Ashley looked down with some uncertainty at the marker in her hands.

"Step one—before firing for the first time," he raised his voice to announce to the entire team, "is to check the setting velocity." He stepped even closer to Ashley—his front close enough to her back to feel her body heat. It wasn't quite as close as they'd been when going over the cargo net on the mock-O-course that morning, but right now he made it far less impersonal by lightly running his hands from her shoulders all the way down her arms—*God damn it, this was not okay, and nope, he would* never *have done that to Clark*—to help her lift the marker into position so she could view the setting.

"Dunk tests all the markers regularly," he loudly continued his lesson even as he started to sweat beneath his mask. Because, yeah, Ashley had stiffened—her shoulders were now up and tight, her body taut. So he pressed a little closer—but upper body only, because Jesus. "We fire each marker into a chronograph that verifies the velocity. So your setting should be locked around 280 for outdoor play. That's feet per second, which translates, again, to about 190 miles an hour. TL, what is your velocity?"

"Two-eighty," she said.

This was where he'd expected her to pull away from him, or to shrug him off, or at least to say or do *something*, but she didn't. She just stood there inside the circle of his arms. So he, too, stayed where he was as he continued, "Check the safety—and it should be on."

It was, but her fingers fumbled as she attempted to flip it, and it was all he could do not to push her hand away and do it for her. Because all he could feel was the smooth heat of her bare arms against the sensitive insides of his own. Thank God she was wearing the kind of mask that had full head cover, or her hair would've been against his neck and cheek. As it was, every breath he took was filled with the sweet scent of her soap and sunblock—even her sweat smelled delicious.

"Okay, safety's off," he could finally announce as he also finally let her go and stepped back. "Aim for the center target."

She glanced back at him over her shoulder before awkwardly hauling the marker up into a ridiculously bad firing position. Her feet were close together, and her shoulders were still up and tight. As soon as she pulled the trigger, the kick of the marker—usually not an issue—pushed her off-balance.

Jim was ready for that—but not ready enough as she stumbled back into him with a full body-slam. She was far less fragile than she looked, with a butt that was as tight and muscular as her runner's thighs. Her abs were equally impressive—while she didn't have a complete six-pack, the softness of both her belly and her smooth skin covered a core that was solid. And yeah, as he'd caught her, mid-flail, her shirt rode up so that his hand accidentally slipped into the gap between it and her jeans.

His right hand. His left wrapped around her in not quite a *full* boob-grab, but pretty damn close.

"Sorry," he said quickly as he made sure she was steady even while he leapt back, away from her. His left hand got entangled between her arm and the marker and he ended up brushing her entire breast with his fingers. "Sorry!"

Christ, after the way he'd touched her arms, she was going to think that was intentional and Jesus, *what* was he doing…?

Except, *she* was apologizing to *him*. "No, sorry, *I'm* sorry!" She'd stepped on his toe, but he'd barely felt it through his boots.

"I'm too far away," she said, and for several weird seconds, Jim had no idea what the hell she was talking about, but then realized that she'd turned to look at the fence.

The paintball she'd fired from her marker hadn't even made it as far as the target. It had landed with a red splash on the small strip of concrete in front of the fence.

He had to clear his throat before he could speak. "No, this is a good distance. If you can only hit your target when you're close to it, you won't stand a chance against the other team. You just have to think about the physics. The relatively low velocity, plus the weight of the pellet..."

"It's like *Angry Birds*," Clark realized. "You know, the video game...? Instead of aiming at where you want the pellet to go, you have to lob it."

Ashley looked over at her brother. "Lob it...?"

The kid's own marker was without air or pellets, but he used it to demonstrate, aiming it up and then using his hand to show the pellet's imagined trajectory—an arc rather than a direct line.

"Let's try it," Jim said. "See what happens. TL...?"

She glanced at him again before moving her marker up to her shoulder, but he stopped her, adding, "This time don't stand like a bowling pin."

As Ashley looked down at her stance, the chatter in the cheap seats continued.

"But doesn't that—lobbing—increase the likelihood of a hit to a target's head?" Kenneth asked, sounding worried. But then again, *worried* tended to be the kid's default. "Isn't that problematic...?"

Jim helped Ashley adjust, his hands back on her shoulders. Again, exactly like he would've done with Clark, except... not... "Feet apart, legs spread," he told her as Bull moaned, "Oh, my God, enough with all of the questions already. No, it's not *problematic*, Queen Mary. It's part of the game. You catch one on your head or your mask, you wipe it, and you keep going."

"A little bit more," Jim told Ashley, using his boot to push her into a wider stance, his leg between hers—*don't think about that, don't think about that...* "Unlock your knees—" he reached down and pushed on the backs of her knees "—lean into it." She leaned too far forward, so he pulled her back. "Not that much. Just a little."

"I was thinking more in terms of the marker-er," Kenneth replied—the conversation going on in the background—the weirdest soundtrack ever, considering Jim's world had shrunk to these few feet of sandy soil that he was sharing with Ashley, to the quiet sound of her breath, to the accelerated beating of his heart, to the warmth of her body against his. It occurred to him that none of them—all male—saw anything wrong with his casual handling of their Team Leader.

Kenneth kept talking. "The shooter, if you will. Potential penalties. And I prefer Queen Elizabeth, thanks."

"Find your balance," Jim told Ashley as he put his hands on the warm softness of her waist. "Use your core." He slid one hand around to cover her stomach, and she just stood there, letting him touch her. He might've touched Clark's stomach, if the kid had been his volunteer, but he probably would've done it with a smack. *Definitely* not a linger… "These are the same muscles you use when you run. You're just using them differently when you're firing a weapon."

"A lob's gonna hurt a lot less than a direct, up-close hit," Clark told Kenneth.

"Can we get to the target practice?" Bull whined. "Some of us already know this shit."

Ashley was still aiming her marker too low, so Jim adjusted for her. "Pull the trigger."

She did, and this time she absorbed the kick—and the pellet landed with an explosion of red directly in the center of the target.

Clark and Kenneth both applauded. Bull and Todd were less impressed. "Great. Now just keep a Navy SEAL glued to your ass throughout the entire game. Oh, wait, maybe that won't be a problem for *you*."

It was only then that Ashley spoke up. "Back off," she said to Jim, then kinda ruined it by politely adding, "Please…?"

But Jim did as she asked, and she raised her marker again—she'd been paying attention, which was remarkable since their close proximity had damn near fried his working brain cells—and fired.

The pellet hit the target—not quite as dead center as when Jim had been helping, but pretty darn close.

But Bull still scoffed. "Beginner's," he said, but before he could utter *luck*, Jim clapped his hands together and loudly announced, "Masks on, markers loaded! Let's go, Team One, let's get you out there!"

CHAPTER TEN

"I've got around fifteen minutes before the first official paintball game starts," Ashley told Colleen, who'd sent her a rather upsetting text.

Sorry to bother you at camp, but there's been a break-in. Call me when you can.

Thank God—at least—that this urgent problem had nothing to do with one of Ashley's many clients, nearly all of whom were women seeking both escape and divorce from abusive spouses.

"Please tell me the break-in was at the office," Ash continued. The law office where she and Colleen worked was in a strip-mall, in a part of town where desperate people often resorted to desperate measures. They'd had break-ins before, and had learned to keep everything of value out and off of their desks, securely locked in a safe.

But Colleen sighed. "Sorry, no, it was your apartment."

Of *course* it was. Her immediate neighbors already were chilly toward her for accidentally parking in their "reserved guest spot," right after moving in. It wasn't theirs—there was no such thing as a reserved guest parking spot, but… whatever. Ash sighed. "How long did the alarm go off? What time did it go off?"

"Yeah, that's the big mystery," Colleen told her. "The alarm *didn't* go off. When I went over this morning, to bring in your mail and water your plants…? I found the door ajar."

"Oh, my God, are you okay? You didn't go inside, did you?" Ashley asked. She looked up to find that her exclamation had brought Lieutenant Slade out of his trailer. But he stopped short, seeing that she was talking on the phone.

"Bobby and Wes were both with me," Colleen said. "Just by chance. They went in while I called 9-1-1. Whoever was in there was already gone."

"Oh, thank God," Ash breathed, opening the screen door and going into her own RV to escape the SEAL's watchful gaze. She'd intended to get up the nerve to talk to him during this relatively

short break. What *was* that, that he'd done—all that touching—out
on the paintball field just a few hours ago? Was that some kind of
Navy SEAL foreplay...? But now that conversation was going to
have to wait until after this afternoon's game, because her freaking
apartment had been freaking broken into.

"It doesn't look like anything was taken," Colleen reported, "but
it's pretty clear that the place has been tossed—you know,
searched...? Drawers got dumped out, and the entire contents of
your freezer was in a puddle on the kitchen floor."

"*What?*"

"Yeah," Colleen agreed. "That was weird, although Bobby and
Wes seem convinced that everyone knows that everyone hides
important things—even money—in their freezers."

"I had some coconut milk ice cream and a six-month supply of
Trader Joe's frozen green beans," Ashley lamented. "From when
they were on sale."

"Not anymore," Colleen said.

"So my TV's still there? And my computer?" Ashley asked,
silently taking a mental inventory of anything of value in her
apartment. "All my clothes are still in my closet?"

"Yeah—I hung everything back up."

"Oh, God, really? My clothes were on the floor...? Is that
weird? It feels weird."

"If I had to guess," Colleen said, "I'd say the perp was either
trying to piss you off or search through all your pockets."

"For what?"

"You tell me," Colleen said.

"I have *no* idea. Crap, I'm almost out of time..."

"Are you really going to play paintball?"

"God help me," Ashley said. "Yes. I'm on a team—a *team*, Col.
This SEAL World thing is entirely about *teams*. Oh, my God, what
am I doing here? But my team is with Clark and Kenneth and two,
no, make that *three* manly-men douche-nozzle types."

"Wait, Clark and Kenneth are there with you...?" Colleen's
voice went up an octave in disbelief.

"Yup. Surprise! Daddy sent Clarkie to... God, I don't even
know why he sent him. Maybe to make sure I don't run off with
some Navy SEAL...?"

"Ooh, what a good idea," Colleen said. "Are there... many
Navy SEALs available for running off with...?

"No," Ashley said. "I mean, I maybe... I mean... I thought Jim was different, but now I'm not so sure..."

"Jim?" Colleen jumped on the name. "Slade? Please tell me it's Jim Slade! Oh my God, Ashley, he's great! I was going to try to set you up with him, but you went to New York, and when you came back you were in your never-gonna-date-again phase."

"It's not a phase," Ashley said. "It's a lifestyle choice. It just makes everything so much easier. I just wish..."

Ash had spent the entire session at the paintball field flashing hot and cold with shock and... something that felt embarrassingly like desire. What was wrong with her?

The more pressing question was, what was wrong with Jim? Somehow—by making penis jokes...? Really...?—Ashley had unwittingly signaled interest in him. Or at least that's how he'd interpreted the fact that she'd sat at his outdoor table making penis jokes. She'd thought she was being funny—instead he'd heard *Come have sex with me.* God, she was an idiot.

And she was double the idiot because she'd liked it. His touch. The warmth of his big hands on her body... So maybe she *had* been saying... that... with those jokes... Except, no, she was pretty sure she hadn't been. But now that he'd brought up the idea, she'd discovered she didn't entirely hate it.

And wasn't *that* an understatement...?

And really, what did it mean about her, that her immediate response wasn't completely appropriate indignation about his disrespect, and was instead mixed with the weakened knees and rapid heartbeats of *Oh, yes please...?*

He was smart. He was funny. And smart and funny always, *always* trumped *hot*, although he was that, too...

"You do know," Colleen said carefully after Ashley's silence had dragged on a bit too long, "that there are plenty of options that don't include the long-term. You could run off with, say, some handy, nearby, totally imperfect, too-manly-man Navy SEAL like Jim for a period of time significantly shorter than a lifetime. A night, for example? Or maybe two...?"

"I *am* aware of that, thanks, but... Should I come home?" Ashley asked.

"What?" Colleen said. "No! Definitely not. I cleaned up the green beans. Also... I don't want to be creepy, but... it might be better if you're *not* here until we find whoever it was who broke in."

"We, Nancy Drew?" Ashley asked. "You and the Hardy Boys?"

"Me, the Hardy Boys—and the police," Colleen corrected her. "Detective Booker wanted me to ask who's got your alarm code, besides me."

"No one," Ashley said.

"Really no one else?" Colleen asked. "Not even Clark? Didn't you give it to him when he and Kenneth came to visit a few months ago?"

"Well, yeah," Ashley said. "But the system allows me to give temporary codes to visitors, and then reset the system after they're gone. And I did. I'm not an idiot." Yeah, actually she was, because her apartment had been broken into, and yet all she could think about was the way Jim had touched her as he'd helped improve her paintball-marker firing stance. That brain-melting warmth of his hand against her stomach... The sparkle of his eyes when he sat outside of his trailer and laughed with her...

"I'm not an idiot either," Colleen said. "I swear, the detective asked me fifteen different times if maybe I'd forgotten to set it, last time I was over here. I finally called the alarm company who verified that it was set at precisely the time I said I'd set it, thank you very much. *And*—this is the extra-bad part: they have a record of it being turned off at around oh-three-hundred—three A.M.—last night."

Three A.M. Usually Ash was sound asleep at three A.M. *That* would've been a really bad surprise... "They should have a record of which code was used," she told Colleen.

"Yeah, it registered as your regular code," Colleen told her. "The one I use."

"And you haven't given that code to anyone...?" Ashley pushed. "Did you write it down or leave it in the office, or—"

"Nope," Colleen confirmed. "I mean, maybe I mumbled it in my sleep, but I really doubt Bobby's the one who broke in to murder your green beans. So, you don't have some kind of online account, where you keep all your passwords or...?"

"No," Ash said.

"Is it possible that... someone who, you know, maybe, um, knows you *really* well might've been able to figure out the combination of numbers—"

"You mean *Brad*?"

"Yes," Colleen said. "Yes, I mean Brad."

"You honestly think it was Brad who broke in?" Ashley asked her friend.

"I still had a picture of the two of you in my phone," Colleen said. "Some of your neighbors have seen him around lately. You know, skulking near your condo door."

Well, that wasn't exactly breaking news. Ashley was here in Florida because *she'd* seen Brad skulking.

"I know you gave him back that giant engagement ring," Colleen said. "But did he give you, I don't know, any other jewelry or…?"

"I gave him back everything," Ash said, and asked again, "You seriously think it was Brad?"

"I'm on the fence, but Bobby and Wes are both convinced. Okay, here's the next question," Colleen said. "Who, besides me, has got a key?"

Jim tried his best not to listen as Ashley told her brother that someone had broken in to her apartment.

"But there was no sign of a forced entry," she reported to Clark as they all waited, once again, outside of the trailer leading into the paintball field. "How they got in is a mystery."

Kenneth was sitting in the shade, looking even more pale than he'd looked just a few hours earlier. Jim made a mental note for Thomas King to take a quick look at the kid when he made his rounds.

"I swear," Clark told her. "I didn't lose your key last time we visited."

"If you ever do again, promise you'll just tell me," Ashley said. "I'd prefer to change the locks *before* someone lets themself into my apartment at three in the morning."

Kenneth spoke up. "I find it hard to believe it's not Brad, considering."

Jim couldn't stop himself from jumping in. "Someone broke into your place at oh-dark-thirty, plus you *know* your ex has been stalking you, and you *don't* think it's him…?"

Ashley's eyes flashed with something—surprise? Annoyance? But it was quickly gone. "Brad's a lawyer," she said. "While he might've been able to guess my password—somehow, maybe, but I really don't know how, unless he bugged my apartment and listened in while I gave it to Colleen—"

"Has Bob or Wes scanned the place for listening devices?" Jim asked.

Ashley laughed. "I was kidding."

"Well, I'm not. The Team's got the gear. Might as well do it." He took out his phone and fired off a quick text to both SEALs.

"I'm pretty sure Colleen and I talked about my security code while we were in the office," Ashley countered.

"A location that's probably even less secure. I'll tell them to scan over there, too."

Ashley sighed her exasperation as she shook her head. "So, Brad suddenly turns into James Bond, plants listening devices and... what...? Goes to lock-picking school?"

"No need. *Hello, Oswald Q. Locksmith...?*" Kenneth pitched his voice lower and did a not-entirely-terrible American accent. "*Yes, my name is Brad Hennesey. I'm locked out of my condo, and my fiancé is out of town. What's that? You only accept cash and it'll cost eight hundred dollars...? No problem. I'll meet you there in ten. No need to replace the lock—there's another key inside, in the junk drawer...*"

Ashley swore.

"You keep a spare key in one of your kitchen drawers, like everyone else in the known universe?" Jim asked.

She nodded. And clearly she was thinking what *he* was thinking, which was that even if Colleen checked to see if that key was still there, the thief could've taken it—after being let in by a locksmith—copied it, and already brought it back, so that they'd think it wasn't missing. "Hello, Oswald Q. Locksmith...? I think I need to change my locks, along with my alarm code."

"Or not," Jim said. "Not yet, anyway. If you want to catch this guy—let's call him *Brad* just for shits and giggles—you should keep everything exactly the same, but add a few hidden mini-cams to your security set up."

"It might've just been someone looking for some quick cash," she argued.

"With this kind of sophisticated entry?" Jim asked. "If the window was broken, sure, but... Come on, you're smarter than that."

She met his gaze steadily. "I *am* smarter than that."

And ooh, she wasn't talking about the break-in. He was pretty certain she was talking about earlier, when he'd had his hands all over her. But she wasn't angry, which was… puzzling.

"All right, all right, all right!" Lucky O'Donlon could do a mean Matthew McConaughey, and he was even more jubilant today, because yes, his wife, Syd, *was* expecting their first baby. It was hard not to smile at his palpable joy. His entire team was behind him as they approached—Team One's rivals for the first paintball game—which was gonna be a bloodbath.

"Consider it," Jim told Ashley. "The cameras."

"I'm considering a lot of things," she said.

Whoa, wait, *what*…? But she'd already turned and was rallying their team—at least Clark and Kenneth. But hey, she'd even gestured for Bull and Todd to join them and they'd moved, albeit reluctantly, into a semi-huddle as Lucky's team went in through the trailer and onto the field.

"The game is elimination," she told them. "Last team standing wins. We've been given this end of the field—the southern half. Lieutenant O'Donlon's team is heading out right now, to open up the trailer in the northern half. When the buzzer sounds, they'll start from way up there, while we start from down here."

"You picked the shitty end of the field," Bull muttered.

"It was a coin toss," Ashley reported. "They got to pick. But I'm okay with it, because we've all spent most of our time on this half, and frankly, we know it best. So here's what we're going to do: Clark, Kenneth, LT, and I are going to hide. Bull and Todd, you're our only hope. You stay out there and do what you do best. Eliminate as many of them as you can."

And there it was. The moment in which Bull and Todd could take Ashley's words of praise, inspired by a famous female general—*You're our only hope*—and rise to the challenge. Join the team.

But Bull remained scornful. "So we're supposed to sacrifice ourselves, so you idiots can win? I don't think so."

Jim felt himself bristle. "You don't have a choice—"

Ashley cut him off. "If any one of us is the last person standing, our entire team wins."

"It's last *man* standing," Bull shot back.

"It probably will be, yes. And that last man will probably be the *real* Navy SEAL," Ashley said crisply. "I'm good with that." She looked over at Jim. "We could use your help, LT, finding the best places for us to hide. I have some ideas, but... Anyway, after we're set, I'll rendezvous with Bull and Todd and let them know exactly where we are. My thought is that if Clark, Kenneth, the LT, and I are scattered, hidden, across the field, we'll have two options. Wait for the enemy to come to us, and if we get a clean shot at any one of them, we'll take it, even if the rest of their team then takes us out. And if we can't get a clean shot, we'll wait for Bull and Todd to lure the other team to where we're hidden, and at your signal, we'll create a diversion—a distraction that will likely get us eliminated, at least those of us who aren't Navy SEALs—but will allow Bull and Todd to eliminate the other team members and win for us all."

It was a basic but pretty brilliant strategy—although the whole suicide-sacrifice approach wouldn't work in a real life scenario. But this was paintball and *dead* wasn't *dead*. It was merely messy with a bit of a sting.

"I have just a few adjustments to TL's plan," Jim said. "I'll get you settled, but *I'll* rendezvous with Bull and Todd. I'll also stay in the field—"

"Your knees—"

"Are fine," he said. *Ah, Christ...* But she didn't argue—even if that same damn word cloud that he imagined also appeared to her. Still, she didn't look happy. "We'll meet at the banyan tree in the southwest corner," he told Bull and Todd. "Fifteen minutes after the start buzzer sounds."

Bull started making noise about the game not lasting more than ten minutes, but Jim cut him off with a sharp, "If you're not there, I'll assume you're already dead. Masks on and into the field." He led the way into the trailer then stood at the door and did his smack-and-yank mask check as the team went out into the yard.

Ashley was last, and this time he didn't do more than the standard, but she just stood there, looking up at him. "Who checks *your* mask?" she asked.

"I do," he said, pulling it down.

But she reached up and smacked-and-yanked anyway—and yeah, he'd forgotten how obnoxious that was. But then she put her hand on his shoulder. It wasn't even close to the way he'd touched her earlier, but despite that, his heart stuttered—just a little. "Don't hurt yourself," she told him quietly. "Don't push too hard. It's just a game."

And with that she went out the door.

★ ★ ★

They were barely five minutes into the game, but deep within the heavily brush-and-pine-treed part of the field, when Kenneth passed out.

One second he was moving quietly along the narrow trail, just behind Jim and in front of Ashley, and the next he was crumpling into the scrub.

At first, Ashley thought he was goofing—but almost immediately she realized that while Clark might've pulled an idiot move like that, Kenneth would never.

"Jim!" She whispered, but he heard her immediately, and was down in the dirt almost before she was, checking Kenneth—holy crap—for a pulse. "Oh, my God, he's burning up." He was radiating heat through his clothes. She turned to glare at her brother. "What the hell, Clark?"

As Jim pulled out his cell phone, Clark crouched on the other side of her, his face panicked through his mask's plastic shield. "Don't look at me! I keep going, *Dude, you look like shit*, and he's all *Celiac, celiac!*"

"Celiac doesn't give you a fever!"

"Cell service appears to be down," Jim announced as he reached to take the Team Leader's bag from Ashley's shoulders.

She wriggled to get free of the strap, shooting him an incredulous look. "Seriously…?"

Jim already had the walkie-talkie out and on, antenna up. "This is why we carry—" He interrupted himself. "Slade to King, do you copy, over? Come in, Corpsman King, over. Hospital corpsman needed at the paintball field, over." He turned up the volume before handing the device to Ashley. "Push this to keep calling for him. Be brief—say *over*, let him answer. Come on, we're gonna get Kenneth back to the trailer."

Ashley immediately got to work. "Team One needs medical assistance, over."

But before Jim could somehow pick Kenneth up, he roused, his eyes fluttering open as he moaned.

"Hey, kid," Jim said, his tone as gently matter-of-fact as if they'd run into each other on the way to the mess. "What's going on?"

"Hurts," Kenneth gasped.

"Where?" Jim asked.

Kenneth's response was to curl into a ball and vomit. Ashley and Clark were both far enough away, but Jim's pants got covered.

He didn't even flinch. "Well, okay," he said in that same quietly calm voice. "I'm gonna go with abdominal pain. Let's get you to the trailer, see if we can't rouse some assistance via the landline."

A landline! In the trailer! "I'll run ahead," Ashley told Jim. "Give me your cell phone. Sir. In case cell service comes back."

"Code to unlock is one oh one oh one oh," he said as he slapped it into her hand. "Go!"

And with that, she was off at a run.

It was probably just a bad case of the flu. Or even food poisoning. And why wasn't Thomas King answering, damn it?

It took far less time to get back to the open clearing by the trailer because she wasn't attempting to be quiet. Still, she managed to completely surprise a cluster of men from Team Three who must've run at full speed down one of the trails along the fence line to get so deeply into Team One's territory so quickly. They'd already hunkered down along the length of fencing that was used for target practice, although they all leaped to their feet when they saw her.

And, like an idiot, she ran toward them. "Oh, thank God, you guys, we need—" *help*.

She didn't get the word out before they all—there were three of them—raised their markers and opened fire.

Sting was not the word she would've used.

Punch was more like it.

Of course, she was heading swiftly toward them, moving well into the verboten three meter no-fire zone. And she did get hit with three pellets at once, all aimed at her center of gravity. And nearly all of the shooters went for overkill with a double pop, so she didn't just get hit once, she got hit again and again.

Ashley hit the ground and the walkie-talkie went skittering out of her grasp. But there wasn't any time to curl into a ball—ow!—or deride herself for not immediately shouting *Hold your fire!* She just scrambled after the walkie-talkie even as she hauled herself back onto her feet.

"Hey, you're dead, you're supposed to stay down," one of the men said, and what the hell? It wasn't some random member of Team Three, it was Bull Edison. And Todd Grotto was standing right beside him.

Sure enough, most of the paint on her shirt was red—her own team's color. Only one of the pellets that had pummeled her was Team Three's yellow.

"Team One is having a medical emergency," Ashley managed to gasp out—those punches to her chest had made her voice sound breathless. "You—Roger!" The Team Three man who'd helped to "kill" her was an older guy—some silver-haired bigwig CEO named Roger Something who was also a marathon runner. "Cell phones are down, and we're having trouble reaching Lieutenant King. Run to the main building—see if he's there. It's Kenneth, the skinny kid from the UK? He's having intense abdominal pain—he passed out. Bull and Todd—what the hell? Don't answer that right now. Because frankly, I don't really care. Just run back along the trail and help LT and Clark get Kenneth to the trailer."

All three of them just stood there, staring at her.

So she clapped her hands at them. "Move! Now!"

Todd cleared his throat. "Bull and I cut a deal with Team Three. So if this is some kind of set-up or trap—"

"If it is," she cut him off, "it's illegal, it won't count, because I'm dead." She pointed to her paint-splattered shirt. "Exhibit A. Okay? Go!"

With that, they went. And Ashley went into the trailer to attempt to reach Lieutenant King via landline.

CHAPTER ELEVEN

"We'll be right behind them," Jim reassured Ashley as the SEAL World van—Dunk behind the wheel with Clark riding shotgun, Thomas King in the back with Kenneth—peeled out down the drive toward the main road that led to Sarasota and the hospital.

"Let's hurry," she said, heading swiftly toward the path to the RVs.

Thomas—when he wasn't apologizing profusely for failing to hear their walkie-talkied request for help—seemed certain that Kenneth's appendix was inflamed, or had even burst.

Kenneth had been desperate for someone to go to his RV, find his phone, and bring it to the hospital so he could get in touch with his parents. Dunk had tried to reassure him that Lieutenants Slade or O'Donlon would call his folks from the SEAL World office, to keep them fully informed of the situation.

But Kenneth's ability to be reasonable was hindered by the intense pain he was experiencing. And he didn't relax until Ashley promised to find his phone and bring it to him. So Jim had likewise volunteered to drive her—which also allowed him to change his puke-encrusted pants.

Now, Ashley slowed as she clearly realized he was struggling to keep up with her.

She dropped a very uncharacteristic f-bomb. "You hurt yourself carrying Kenneth down the trail, didn't you?"

"I'm okay." No way would she have bought *fine*. Not from the way he was limping. "Are *you*?" From the amount of paint on her shirt, she'd walked—no, probably run—straight into an ambush. Although...

"I'm not the one with a potentially burst appendix," she pointed out, "so I'm kind of great."

Jim smiled. "Yeah, good way to look at it. Me, too. But I'm not sure why you're covered in red paint. I mean, yellow's in there, but..."

"Bull and Todd went turncoat," she informed him. "Can they

even do that? Is that even a real thing in paintball?"

He caught her arm at the fork between their two RVs. "Are you telling me that *Bull and Todd* shot you…?"

She nodded.

"I'm gonna freaking kill 'em."

Her smile was beautiful, if over too quickly. "Thanks, but you don't have to. I'm okay."

"Those things can bruise."

"I thought they only *stung*."

"Can I see? I want to see. Lift your shirt."

Her eyebrows went up.

Jim refused to back down. He waited. He knew he could out-wait damn near anyone.

"Usually, I like to kiss a man first," she said. "*Before* I flash him."

It was meant to be a joke, but he was not in the mood. "Great," he said. "Let's do this, then."

And he lifted her chin, leaned down, and covered her mouth with his.

Her lips were soft and warm and he could practically taste her surprise—although maybe that was his, because holy Jesus not only was he kissing her, but after that initial moment of *Whoa*, she was kissing him back.

Soft turned to something else—which wasn't to say that her lips weren't still deliciously soft, but they were suddenly something more, too. Something that matched the way her arms went up around his neck and the way her body was suddenly pressed against his. That was all her, not him, although it was a damn good idea, and he immediately responded in complete freaking agreement and wrapped his arms around her, too.

He knew—from his earlier manhandling—that her strong runner's legs led to an equally strong torso and core. But the fact that she was a perfect mix of soft and solid against him was still a surprise, as was her hunger for more.

That was what he was feeling—*hunger*—from her lips and her arms…

But just as suddenly as she'd started kissing him back, she stopped. She pushed herself away from him, and Jim quickly let her go.

"No," she said, although the word didn't match the glaze of

desire in her eyes. Except she shook her head, and said it again. "No."

"Sorry." That was her word, and he winced because it was no less pathetic coming out of his mouth.

"No," she said again and this time she seemed to be disagreeing with his *Sorry*, but he wasn't sure because his entire world was still on a rather drastic tilt. "We have to hurry. Change, and then head back toward the mess. I'll catch up tó you after I find Kenneth's phone."

"Won't you need help?" Jim asked. Clark had said that the camper he and Kenneth were sharing was a mess as he'd given them the keypad code, and he wasn't sure where Kenneth kept his phone. "Searching through the rubble...?"

But Ashley was already sprinting toward her own RV. "No, I'm going to use my phone to call his phone when I'm in there."

"Brilliant," Jim called after her as he made his way to his own trailer door. "And I *am* sorry. I don't really know *what* that was..."

But she was already inside, the screen door slapping closed behind her.

Jim left his pants outside his own door and went in to quickly change into his cargo shorts.

The drive into Sarasota was awkward.

Ashley had been counting on having a full thirty minutes alone with Jim to discuss that mind-blowing kiss. Instead, there was no chance to talk, because the SUV's backseat was filled with three campers who were heading to the airport. *Something had come up at work*—AKA, they were quitting the session. Dunk hadn't been kidding about SEAL World's high dropout rate.

The three men—all CEOs in their late forties, two named Peter and one named Bruce—were completely packed and ready to go. Ash knew that if they hadn't been ready, Jim wouldn't have waited for them. As it was, he made it very clear that he was going straight to the hospital—they would have to find their way to the airport from there.

He, too, was annoyed by their presence—and Ashley wasn't sure if that was a good sign or a bad sign. Although it was generally her experience that a person didn't apologize immediately after a kiss if they liked it and wanted to do it again.

Although, to be fair, *she* was the genius who'd shouted *No* in his face when what she'd really meant was *Wow, that was lovely but super distracting, so let's not plan to do that again until some time way out in the future, because right now we really have to get to the hospital ASAP to be there for both Kenneth and Clark.*

So it was possible that Jim's current annoyance was also aimed at Ashley—or maybe it was just from the fact that his knees were hurting him.

He'd brought along ice for them—except he hadn't, not really. It turned out the ice was for her—so she could soothe the welts from those paintball pellets. He didn't ask to see them again, no doubt only due to the full backseat. He just assumed they were there—which they were.

Ashley had gotten a quick look when she'd changed her paint-splattered clothes. She had a mix of marks—the worst was a purple-red bruise right below her collarbone—but most of the others were already starting to fade. It was obvious that the extra layer of her running bra had protected her—the marks on her chest were far less severe.

As she'd finally surrendered and slipped the wrapped bag of ice up under her shirt, Jim had shot her both a look and a quick little wry smile.

That was promising.

But before she could murmur, *We need to talk later*, the SUV's Bluetooth screen lit up with a call to Jim's cell from *TK*—which turned out to be Thomas King.

"It's definitely Kenneth's appendix," the young lieutenant announced over the car's speaker phone. "But it hasn't yet burst, which is great news. It means they'll go in laparoscopically, which is far less invasive. He's being prepped for that surgery right now."

"Oh, thank God," Ashley said. "Thank you for calling to tell us that."

"Team Leader DeWitt," Thomas continued, "I owe you an apology for being unavailable via walkie-talkie. There was no one at the range, and I was unaware that there was an issue with cell service out on the paintball field. I was on another phone call myself—Tasha, that girl I was telling you about...? She got into some trouble, and her uncle called to see if maybe she'd reached out to me. Anyway, I wrongly assumed that if there was a problem at camp, I'd see the incoming call and be able to switch over immediately. That's not meant to be an excuse, ma'am, merely an explanation for my distraction and resulting negligence. Again, I'm deeply sorry."

"It's okay, Lieutenant," Ashley told him. "Roger found you quickly enough." Thomas had made it out to the paintball field's south trailer just as Jim had gotten Kenneth there. "How's Clark doing? And has anyone contacted Kenneth's parents?"

"I'm hanging with Clark in the waiting room right now," Thomas reported. "He's okay. Less worried now that we know Kenneth's risk of complications is much lower. Dunk called Kenneth's folks—they're flying in. I think they're already on their way."

"That's great," Ashley said. "Please let Clark know that we'll be there soon. GPS says twenty minutes."

Thomas promised that he and Dunk would stay with Clark at least until she and Jim arrived, and signed off.

Someone in the back said, "There's always a distraction with them, isn't there? And it's always some girl."

With *them*...? Ashley turned around to look at the three men—all white, all born into wealth, all quitting the relatively easy SEAL World program. She purposely misunderstood, and kept her voice light. Pleasant. A tad condescending. "This girl is the teenaged niece of a high ranking naval officer, who happens to be a dear family friend of Lieutenant King—so his *distraction* is understandable and appropriate. I know what you meant, though. Men *do* tend to be more easily distracted than women, that's true, but Navy SEALs usually deal with it better than most."

Jim may have laughed, but he turned it into a cough, and when she glanced back at him, his eyes were glued to the road in front of them.

The man who'd spoken—the older Peter—was unwilling or unable to let her appropriate his word, *them*. Or maybe it was being schooled by a woman that chafed. "No need to get your panties in a twist, sweetheart. I'm just saying that boy's apology's a thing of art."

Jim looked sharply into his rearview. "I'm sorry, what?"

Ashley turned around again, but Peter was now silent.

"One of you quitting motherfuckers just called a Team Leader *sweetheart*, and a Navy SEAL officer a *boy*," Jim said as he jerked the wheel hard to the right and pulled off onto the shoulder of the road with a spray of gravel. They were still in the middle of nowhere. Cattle grazed to the left, and a citrus orchard was off to the right. "Whoever just said that better start groveling, or I'll leave all of you right here, at the side of the road."

The older Peter cleared his throat. "No disrespect intended."

"Bullshit," Jim fired back. "Apologize to Team Leader DeWitt."

Peter chuckled. "Ah, of course. I apologize, *Team Leader* DeWitt."

And there it was. The look he gave Ashley, with that knowing smile…? It was filled with the assumption that Jim was sleeping with Ashley—that this was the only reason why Jim was adamant Peter show her the proper respect.

"Try it again, *sweetheart*," Jim said. "Without the air-quotes around *Team Leader*."

"Oh, for the love of God!"

Bruce leaned closer. "Just do it, Peter."

"What, you really think he's going to just dump us on the side of the road?" Peter asked.

"He might," the other Peter chimed in. "And then we'll miss our flight."

Peter sighed heavily. "I apologize, Team Leader DeWitt."

"I'll take it," Ashley quietly told Jim. "Let's go. Clark needs us."

"One more for Lieutenant King," Jim ordered.

"My apologies to Lieutenant King."

Jim shook his head as he pulled back onto the road with another spray of gravel. "I'll pass that along," he said as he looked hard into the rearview mirror. "Like Team Leader DeWitt, Lieutenant King is ten thousand times the man you are. And you? *Boys* in the back who didn't call out your buddy's misogyny and racism when it first dribbled from his bullshit-spouting lips…? Fuck you, too. And don't worry, I'll include the details of this entire conversation in my report to Senior Chief Duncan."

CHAPTER TWELVE

The hospital had valet parking.

Which meant Jim could swiftly walk away from the SUV without punching anyone in the face. Ashley didn't say as much, but it was clear to him she was happy about that—but no doubt only because she didn't have the time or inclination to bail him out of jail after he was arrested for assault.

But it also meant that she followed him directly from a crowded SUV to a crowded hospital waiting room, where again, any private discussion had to be curtailed.

Sorry about that kiss. I went too far, I know, but in all honesty, I don't understand why you're willing to defend other people but not yourself...? Peter Asshole calls Thomas King boy and boom, you're ready to throw down. I mean, you were plenty polite—sure—at least at first, which is a fine strategy. I've seen you stand up for your brother and Kenneth, too. So maybe I've been going about this wrong—trying to push you to get so angry that you lose it—thinking that it's anger you've got a problem with. Maybe it's not about getting angry. Maybe it's about buying into the myth that things are never gonna change when it comes to the way people treat you... So you walk away from a battle you believe you can't win...

Things Jim didn't say as he sat in that hospital waiting room.

Kenneth's surgery went well but it took seemingly forever. When the doc finally came out to announce that the kid was in the recovery room and doing well, Dunk and Thomas started making noise about returning to camp.

"I can drive the SUV back," Ashley suggested so that Jim could go with them.

"Nah, I'll stay," he said.

She didn't argue.

But then it was Ash, Clark, and Jim in the waiting room—waiting for Kenneth to be moved to a room where they could sit with him until his parents showed up—and Clark was still a mess.

"I should've known it wasn't celiac," he kept saying.

So Jim drew the kid into a conversation. SEAL 101. "How's your writing?" he asked.

Clark blinked. "My what?"

"Your writing," Jim repeated. "You any good at it? And I'm not talking about the sci-fi novel you started back in seventh grade that you keep on some old flashdrive, although that's cool, too. I'm talking report-writing. Can you do it quickly and easily, or does it make your head explode?"

Clark glanced at Ashley, but she shrugged. She didn't know where Jim was going, either. "I don't hate it," he said, "but I don't exactly love it."

"You got any electives left before you graduate?" Jim asked.

It was another question that made Clark exchange a bemused look with his sister. She shrugged again.

"I'm getting a liberal arts degree," he said, "so..."

"That would be a *yes*," Jim said. "Good. Take an old-school journalism course. Intro or basics. Who, what, when, where, how, and sometimes even why. Read some Ernest Hemingway and channel his style. Short sentences, direct and to the point. If you can learn to write a report quickly, you'll be miles ahead of the game. For example, this evening, both your sister and I are going to have to write up reports about what happened out on the paintball field with Kenneth, *and* about what happened in the car while we were driving to the hospital."

It was clear that Clark still didn't know what report-writing had to do with him, but he was immediately intrigued. "What happened in the car...?"

"We gave a ride," Ashley said, "to three campers who were leaving SEAL World."

"In my version of the report, I'm going to refer to them as *the quitters*," Jim interjected. "It'll make it a little more brief and to the point."

"And one of them made a comment about Lieutenant King—"

"A disparaging comment," Jim added.

"At that point in the conversation, that was open to interpretation," Ashley said, "so that won't go into my report. But he definitely *them*-ed the lieutenant. It wasn't quite a full *those people*, but it was close—"

"So Team Leader DeWitt responded to his comment," Jim continued, "as if he'd meant *all men* with his douchebaggy *them*—

not just the ones who aren't, you know, blindingly white."

Ashley looked at him. "Will you be using *douchebaggy* in your report, Lieutenant?"

He managed to keep a straight face as he nodded. "That or *asshole-ish*. I haven't quite made up my mind about that word choice yet."

She nodded—she, too, was working hard not to laugh. "The man in question—"

"The douchebaggy quitter." Jim interrupted her again. "Yeah, that rings right. I'm definitely using that."

That one broke her. "*The douchebaggy quitter*," she repeated as she laughed, "attempted to put me in my place by calling me *sweetheart*, and then ended up referring to Lieutenant King as *that boy*, clarifying his racist meaning of his previously-used *them*, and causing Lieutenant Slade to respond by slamming on the brakes and threatening to leave all three previously mentioned quitters at the side of the road."

"Oh, my God," Clark was wide-eyed and grinning. "I wish I'd been there."

"It was rather wonderful," Ashley said. "I was impressed."

Really...? "Subjective opinions generally stay out of reports," Jim pointed out.

"Generally," Ashley agreed. "But in this case, your actions were in direct support of both Lieutenant King—and me. I want to make sure, first, that Dunk understands that, and secondly, that both you and he know how very much I appreciated what you did and said. Speaking up is important. It matters."

Jim was sitting there, grinning at her like an idiot, and she was smiling back at him, and okay, yeah, he was supposed to be distracting Clark. He cleared his throat and said, "Well, okay," as he turned back to the kid. He cleared his throat a second time. Where was he before they were sidetracked... Ah, *writing skills*. "That was the deciding factor, for me—to join the Navy as an officer—the fact that writing is one of my strengths. And I'm not saying I like it, either, but I can definitely get it done efficiently. And that's important because officers and enlisted go through BUD/S—SEAL training—together. The challenges are the same for all SEAL candidates—it's honestly the hardest thing I've ever done—but the officers also have to be, well, officers. And that means we write reports, if reports need to get written. Same goes after you're a

SEAL. You get back from training, or even an op, and everyone showers and goes out for a beer, except not so fast there you—because the officers need to write up their reports."

"Why would anyone want to be an officer?" Clark asked, but then answered his own question. "Because you're in command."

"Ding," Jim said. "Also, the uniforms are prettier."

"What do you wish you knew," Ashley asked, "before you went through BUD/S? I mean, what do you know now—what have you learned—that would've helped you as a... you called it a *SEAL candidate*...?"

"Yeah, candidate, and that's... a very good question," Jim said. "I would say... Go in knowing your strengths, and your weaknesses. Know what you're good at—as well as what you're not. Be realistic about it. And then find the guys who can't do what you can, and help them. And the ones who learn to turn around and do the same for you—to help you with the challenges that *they* can do well but you can't...? They're the ones you keep close. They'll be your teammates for life."

Clark was nodding. Ashley had never seen her brother listening quite so intently.

"Because think of it like this," Jim said. "Okay. First, the best mindset for going into BUD/S is to be open to everything. And to recognize that it's attitude that's going to get you through the program. Too many people focus on the physicality. Yeah, you need to be strong, and you need to be fast, well, fast enough. I'm one of those fast-enough guys—or I was, once-upon-a-time. But my strength is that I don't quit. I may not win the race, but I can run forever—or I could. You know, before Knees-mageddon...? I can still swim forever. Again, I'm not winning the race, but if you need someone to cross the channel with only a pair of fins, I'm your man.

"At the same time, when I'm making a team for an op, I'm gonna look for someone who *is* fast—like Rio Rosetti or your sister, here." He pointed to Ashley. "And I'm gonna want a hospital corpsman along for the ride, like Thomas King. A chief like Dunk. A gear-head, a sniper, a languages expert... Everyone's got a skill—a strength—that makes them elite. And yeah, we can all shoot, and swim, and run, and we all know first aid, and most of us have at least two other languages we can use to communicate in a pinch. But when you put us together, into a seven or eight man team...? We're the very best of all of us. We're unstoppable.

"Now," he said, "when you go into BUD/S, there's a tendency for guys to connect—to become friends—with like-minded guys. Gear-heads find other gear-heads. Snipers hangout with other snipers. But if you're an officer, you should go into the training looking for the enlisted man who's gonna be your chief. Of course there're no guarantees you'll end up in the same SEAL Team, but you might. And friendships forged in BUD/S are unbreakable."

"Thank you."

"You're... welcome...?" Jim seemed surprised and not entirely certain what Ashley was talking about as they waited for the hospital valet to bring up their car.

Kenneth's parents and his twin sister, Louise, had finally arrived, and all of them—Clark included—were finally allowed in to see Kenneth. Clark wanted to stay overnight at the hospital, and Kenneth's mom, Mary, was happy to share that job with him. It was clear that she adored Clark.

But now it was well after midnight.

Jim had insisted on paying the parking fee, and Ashley had been too exhausted to argue.

They finally were alone—for the first time since he'd kissed her.

Since she'd kissed him. Fair was fair. He may have started it, but she'd taken it and run.

"Thank you for taking Clark at his word," she said now, as they stood in the wiltingly humid Florida night. "You didn't say *if* you're serious about becoming a SEAL or *if* you're really going to go to BUD/S. You just... spoke to him like you believed him."

"I *do* believe him," Jim said.

She smiled at him. "Thank you for that."

He smiled back at her. "Watching you with Clark was... Well, you're his sister, but you're also, kind of, his mom."

"He was a baby when our mother died."

"Which means that you must've been a baby, too. He's not *that* much younger than you."

"Ten years," she said. "Huge difference between twelve and two."

"That must've been..." Jim shook his head. "I'm so sorry. I mean, my mom still sends me care packages. I don't see her that often, but it's nice to know that she and Dad are always just a phone call away."

"You should go home to visit them while your knees heal," Ashley said. She laughed. "Although, I don't even know where you're from."

The valet arrived with the camp SUV. "Everywhere and nowhere," Jim told her as he opened the passenger side door for her. "Dad was Navy, too. We moved around a lot. Right now they're in Santa Fe. My sister's there, she's got a coupla kids. They're doing the grandparent thing."

"That could be fun. Visiting them...?" Ashley said as he climbed behind the wheel.

The look he shot her was filled with amusement. "You and I have different definitions of *fun*." He pulled out onto Tamiami Trail—the main road, heading south. There wasn't much traffic this time of night and it wouldn't take them long to get back to the camp.

Ashley cleared her throat. *About that kiss...* But when she opened her mouth, she couldn't say the words. Besides, she was curious. "So... where do you think of as *home*?" she asked instead.

"Wherever the Teams are," he said without hesitation. But then he laughed. "I guess I learned early on that *home* isn't a place—an apartment or a house or even any specific town or city. That was always temporary—and it still is. Give me a tent and a bedroll, and I'll be happy. I mean, yeah, a toilet and a shower's always nice, but... When I was a kid, the only truly consistent thing in my life was the ocean—the smell of the spray, the sound of the waves, that mind-expanding stretch of the endless horizon. God, it's still... It's where I can breathe. So, oddly enough, I'm most grounded on a ship with no land in sight."

Ashley realized that she'd been holding her breath—his words had been so heartfelt and even poetic. "That's amazing that you know that. You know, about yourself. That's..." It wasn't just poetic—it was profound. "I don't think I've ever felt grounded. Not like that."

After her mother had died, they'd moved. Closer to the city so her father's commute was shorter. To a house that had accommodations for a live-in nanny.

It had been such a stupid, unnecessary accident. Her mother had been home alone. Ashley had been at some god-awful overnight ballet retreat, Clark had gone next door to the neighbors' for a playdate, and her father had been out of town on business. Mom had been storing her gardening tools in the garage for the winter, and one of the hooks in her pegboard must've come out, because she'd gotten out the ladder, probably to try to fix it. She must've lost her balance because she fell and hit her head on the concrete floor. The neighbor had finally called the police at six o'clock, after Mom was two hours late to pick up Clark. Mom was still alive when they found her and rushed her to the hospital, but... it was too late, her head injury had become too severe in the time that she'd been lying there, and they couldn't save her.

Ashley hadn't blamed her father for not wanting to live in that house where her mother had died, but for her, nowhere else had ever felt like home again. But it wasn't the house, it was the fact that her mom was gone.

"Home is where the heart is," she murmured. Except, she'd lost her heart too many times.

Jim was nodding. But then he cleared his throat. "Hey, can I, um, bring up an, uh, awkward-ish topic...?"

She glanced at him, knowing immediately what was coming. "Of course."

"I'm sorry about before," he said. "I shouldn't've kissed you. As your instructor that's... well, you're here to learn from me. And yeah, you're the team leader, but I hold the position of power. I'm sure I violated about a dozen of Dunk's rules, but more importantly, I stepped all over my own code of ethics and, you know, honor. So that was not okay, and, uh, well, I really do apologize."

Ashley nodded silently because *It's okay, because I really didn't mind* was not the right response to their both having broken a SEAL World rule, with all of its potentially legally fraught implications. And yet, her time here was up in just a few short days. But before she could find the words to point that out, he continued.

"And after your session's over," he said and she started nodding, because, yes, after this was over, they'd both be back in the greater San Diego area, "I would really, *really* like to—"

And here it came. *Meet you for coffee, take you out to dinner, kiss you again until our clothes fall off and I'm deep inside of you, making you come...* "God, I would really like that, too," she said in a rush, speaking over him.

Except that *wasn't* what he was saying. "—use you as a resource as I feel my way through maybe making the decision to go to

SEAL CAMP   107

law school. Oh, good. I'm glad you're okay with that. I mean, someday, right? I'm still hoping for a few more years with the Teams, but my expiration date is definitely approaching. And I like you, I do, you're incredible—you're smart and funny and... But my track record is abysmal and... I want us to stay friends, Ashley, and I definitely don't want to mess that up by starting something that can't last."

Oh, God. Oh, crap... "Of course," Ash heard herself say instead of *No—are you crazy...? With heat like that, who cares if it lasts...?* Except, she *did* care. And as long as she didn't look at it directly, she could pretend that she cared—like Jim—about staying friends with him. Instead of caring about it lasting in a *They lived happily ever after* kind of way.

But, now that they'd decided to be friends, she could ask him, as his alleged friend: "So you have a bad track record, too, huh?"

The look he shot her was a mix of amusement and chagrin. "Terrible. I suck as a boyfriend—or so I've been told at rather high volume. It's just not in my skill set to, well, suffer fools gladly." He winced. "Which is not to say the women I've dated are fools. That's not how I meant that. I just... I tend to choose badly, without looking beyond the, you know, shiny... outer... pretty... Which, when I say it out loud, means that *I'm* the fool, or... Maybe, you know, my picture should be in the official idiom's guide, next to the entry for *Love is blind*. Or *Lust is blind*. Yeah, cause, you know..." He cleared his throat. "But then reality catches up to me and... Everyone I fall for turns out to be, well, a little crazy. Not, like, capable-of-stalking-me crazy, though. Which reminds me. I got a text from the Chief—Bob Taylor. He told me you OKed his request to put a coupla security cameras at your place, so I gave him a little guidance as to what and where—I hope you don't mind."

"No," she said. "That's... great."

"One's inside, in your living room, and one's right outside the front door. Both small and hidden. It was cheap and easy—and connected to your wireless. You can watch 'em through an app on your phone. Here." He handed her his cell. "I set up the account and tried it out while we were in the waiting room, while you went to find food. It comes with a free month of digital recording—that's where it gets pricey. The monthly fee to keep the camera's footage for longer than a few hours is pretty steep... But it's free for this trial period and... Hopefully we'll catch this guy before you fly back home."

Ashley opened the app on his phone. And there it was. Two little windows to her life back in California. The first was labeled "A's front door," and it let her see the outside covered corridor that led to her second floor apartment, warmly lit by the overhead lighting. The second was "A's LR," and yup, there was her tidy little living room. Bobby must've left the light on over by the door, because that room was lit, too—and it was already night on the west coast.

"Thanks for doing this," she murmured to Jim.

"Not a problem," he said. "In fact, it's kinda my wheelhouse. Gotta let me bring something to this friendship, right?"

"Yeah," Ashley said and somehow managed to smile.

Friendship. Right.

CHAPTER THIRTEEN

The party in the lounge—an impromptu celebration of Lucky's good news that his wife Syd was indeed pregnant—had wound way down. Jim held the door for Ashley, then followed her in.

The father-to-be was nowhere in sight. He had, apparently, already called it a night. In fact, the youngsters—Thomas and Rio—were alone at the bar. Except, no. Douches one and two—Bull and Todd—were also there, huddled at the table in the corner. Jesus, confronting them about firing on their own team leader during the paintball game was the dead last thing Jim wanted to do right now.

Please God, let them have the good sense to leave…

But although they sat up, they didn't stand. So Jim sighed and kept them in his peripheral as he went behind the bar—first things first.

"Glass o' your favorite grape-flavored beer-substitute, TL?" he asked as he glanced at Ashley, not wanting to assume.

"Oh, God, yes, please," she said. "The pinot noir. Thank you. LT."

That pause before *LT* was tiny and possibly a figment of his imagination. TL and LT. Look at them both being the *exact* right amount of casual-friendly. Since that *was* what he'd said he wanted, why did it annoy him?

As he poured her wine, Ashley turned to Thomas. For her, *first things first* meant asking, "Any word on your friend's missing niece?"

"Yeah," the young SEAL said, clearly surprised that with all the drama around Kenneth, she'd remembered. "Thank you—yes. They found her—well, actually, she called them. To say she's staying with a friend, and that she's safe."

"Oh, I'm so glad," Ashley said.

Thomas smiled his relief as he nodded. "Yeah."

Not wanting to be left out, Rio chimed in. "Thanks for keeping us posted from the hospital. I'm glad Ken's surgery went okay."

"He's doing well. Turns out his parents were visiting his sister in New Orleans, and they caught a flight to Orlando and drove down. I was imagining them flying in from London, but they were closer than that. Anyway, happy ending, they're with Kenneth now. Clark, too. He's still at the hospital," Ashley said as she reached to take her glass of wine from the bar, briefly meeting Jim's eyes with a smile and a "Thanks. LT."

Nah, he was definitely not imagining that slight pause before LT—as if she'd remembered just a little too late that they were only friends, so she added it to make sure she didn't come across as *too* friendly.

And again, his annoyance spiked. Especially as she added, "Shall we sit?" as she motioned toward one of the little cafe tables close to the bar, so they could still talk to Thomas and Rio, but so that Jim could also be comfortable. Bar stools weren't conducive to elevating feet—which is something he definitely needed to do to at least attempt to ease the ache in his knees. She was thinking of him, as always.

"Do you need ice?" she asked, and yes, he did, but there it was again. "LT?"

Thomas leapt into action. "I'll get it, sir."

"No, no, no," Jim said, stopping the younger SEAL, because he suddenly couldn't bear it another second—he had to get the hell out of there. "Email's been weird on my phone—" not a lie, in fact he'd whined about it at least three different times at the hospital "—I should probably go check it on Dunk's computer. I'll get some ice while I'm over there and, you know..."

Checking his email was around fifty thousand on his list of things he actually wanted to do at 0100 after a long, *long* day, but he could not sit there and pretend he wasn't as annoyed as hell by Ashley's attempt to give him exactly what he'd asked for—her friendship.

Because he knew, with that *Let's be friends* speech he'd given her back in the SUV, that he'd disappointed her—but not enough, apparently, to challenge him, or to fight for what she wanted. And that pissed him off. Of course, it was also possible that she didn't consider him truly worth fighting for...

She was now studying the wine in her glass, her face expressionless.

It was Thomas who shot Jim an almost comical WTF questioning look as Rio immediately moved down from his bar stool to join

Ashley at her table.

Jim shook his head—just a miniscule movement—even as he sent Thomas back an answering look that clearly said, *Do not leave her alone with the idiots over there in the corner.* He glanced at Rosetti. *Or with Rio, for that matter.* Jesus.

Thomas was clearly puzzled, but he nodded.

"I better get to it," Jim said aloud, but Ashley was already giving Rio her full attention—exactly the way she did when she spoke to anyone.

And as he took his beer and limped his way out of the lounge, he realized that he and Thomas were nearly as bad as Bull and Todd when it came to the way they treated Ashley. As if a woman wasn't a person, but rather a… well, one word for it was *possession*, some *thing* that two men would discuss silently over the top of her head, without her knowledge.

Yeah, both Jim and Thomas were concerned for Ashley's safety, but the true subtext of their silent conversation went like, Thomas: *Wait, what, you're gonna check email instead of chilling with this gorgeous woman who is clearly into you, whom you're clearly into, too, I mean, really, sir…?*

Jim: *You're wrong. I don't want her.*

Thomas: *You crazy, but okay…*

Jim: *Babysit her for me, though. I don't want her, and I know you don't either, because* you *crazy, too, but let's treat her like a total child who needs to be protected not just from assholes like Bull and Todd, but from her own potential choices because we both know that Rio's certainly not right for her, but God forbid we trust Ashley to make that decision for herself…*

As he went out the door, she laughed at something Rio said, and Jim glanced back to see that Thomas had joined them at the little table.

I don't want her. Jesus, he was a goddamned liar.

And the wave of longing that hit him as he limped through the dimly lit mess hall was now more than mere annoyance. It was heartbreaking, because Ashley was different. Or rather, *he* was different. Yeah, she was pretty and she'd caught his eye from the start, but unlike his MO of the past—thanks only to the structure of SEAL World, to be clear—Jim hadn't immediately jumped into bed with her. Instead, over these past few days, he'd gotten to know her, and he honestly liked her. He saw her clearly—as the strong but flawed woman she was—and he wanted her not despite that but because of it.

The truth was, if he had been at a different place in his career— if, like Thomas and Rio, his time with the Teams stretched out seemingly endlessly in front of him—he would've risked it. *Hey, I gotta be honest. I suck at relationships—or at least I have in the past. And we really can't hook up here, cause, you know, I don't want to mess with Dunk's rules about fraternizing, but how about, after we get back to California, we make plans to connect...?*

The truth was, Jim's time with the Teams was running out. He'd been telling himself it was down to years, but in reality, he knew he should adios that optimistic plural and make it *year.* Maybe. If he got lucky.

But the real truth was, upon his return to San Diego, he was going to get called into his CO's office, and Captain Catalanotto was going to give him The Talk. Which would include the words *Perhaps it's time to move into the next phase of your life.*

The next phase of his far more sedentary, dull-as-a-doornail, neither action-packed nor adventurous, non-Navy SEAL, middle-aged-leading-ploddingly-to-his-death life.

Christ.

Because that was going to suck. *He* was going to suck. And no way was Jim willing to shove the hot mess that he was about to become into Ashley's lap. Like she needed someone else to take care of.

And yeah. He could pretend he was being all selfless and strong for her sake, but the ultimately real and very sad truth was that he was afraid.

He was freaking terrified that she would treat him the same way he'd treated all of his less-than-perfect girlfriends-past. That as soon as she realized she hadn't gotten the strong and shiny Navy SEAL officer, but instead had the washed up ghost of an angry, frustrated, and aimless ex-SEAL, she'd drop him—appropriately—like a stone. Or a doornail—because really, WTF was a doornail, anyway...?

Jim limped into Dunk's office and slapped on the overhead light. He didn't really want or need to check his email, but he'd said he was going to, so he was going to. He sat down—ow, his knees— and woke up the computer on Dunk's desk and...

He'd thought his evening couldn't get any worse, but there it was. As if he'd conjured it from the dark, dank recesses of his toxic imagination.

His depressing future had arrived in the form of an email from a Navy counselor named Lieutenant Westland who wanted to set up a time to discuss where Jim thought he might go from here.

Here was not defined. And in typical military SNAFU format, the various reports and medical evaluations that the counselor cited were not attached.

Jim sifted quickly through his email, but there was nothing else from a dot mil address—nothing from his CO, Captain Joe Catalanotto, either.

Really, this piece of devastating news should have come from Joe Cat—who was CCed on this email—Jim leaned in and squinted at the date and time at the top—which had been sent just an hour ago. Although it *was* very clear from the counselor's use of the words *the next phase* of Jim's *career in the U.S. Navy,* that the word *here* directly pertained to his recent medical evaluation.

Jim sat back in Dunk's chair. It was over.

He was over and done.

And really, wasn't it *dead* as a doornail...?

But he wasn't dead yet, so he reached for his phone, quickly doing the time-zone math. It was after 2200 in California, which was crossing the line, but he dialed Captain Catalanotto's personal cell anyway. Can't kill a man who's already doornail-dead....

The CO picked up on the first ring—caller ID clearly in play. "Hey, Space, what's happening? Everything all right?" His voice was warm and welcoming—and he clearly had no clue.

Jim hadn't woken him—that was good. The captain told him he was watching a movie with his wife, Veronica, but that was okay—they'd hit pause.

Still, tick tock. Jim filled him in as quickly as possible—and got a resounding "What the *hell*...?" as Joe Cat quickly went to check his own email.

"I'm sorry to bother you, but I haven't seen any of the medical evals or the reports being cited," Jim told his CO. "I was hoping you had 'em, so I could see if there's even a chance of, well... A chance."

"I haven't seen anything," Joe said grimly. "And there's nothing here, but... Ah, here's that email from Ron Westland, hold on..." He swore again as he read through it. "Lieutenant, this is *not* the way this should have been handled, you deserve better than this—

and I apologize."

"Sir, this isn't your fault. I know that. I just was hoping..."

"For more info, yeah. Me, too. Let me make a phone call or two—"

"It's kinda late," Jim started.

"I don't give a damn," Joe said flatly. "I'll wake up the admiral if I have to. I'm gonna get us both copies of everything tonight. You deserve to know exactly what's going on, and whether we can fight it, or..." He exhaled hard. "Jim, this is bullshit. I'll call you right back."

And with that, he hung up, leaving Jim sitting there, in Dunk's office, thinking about that *Whether we can fight it, or...*

Because he knew the word that came next was *not*.

Ashley left the lounge, half-looking for Jim, but mostly because she had to use the ladies' room.

The light was on in Dunk's office—he was no doubt still in there. She was hesitant to interrupt him—so she went down the hallway that led to the unisex *head*—as the bathroom was called aboard a boat.

Or ship.

There was a definite difference between the two, according to size, and it was not okay to call a boat a ship or vice versa, so when in doubt use *seagoing vessel*. She'd just been discussing that, in a lively conversation with Thomas and Rio, during which a few too many bars of the theme song to *Love Boat* had been sung.

Rio had a surprisingly lovely voice—rich and husky. And the warm twinkle in his dark brown eyes should've been an ego-boost.

She'd laughed along with them, of course—but all the while she was hyper-aware that Jim hadn't yet returned to the lounge. And hadn't returned. And *still* hadn't returned. So she'd also been kicking herself. For kissing the man, and for not being honest when they'd discussed it in the car.

And for letting herself like him enough, in the first place, so that she was hurt by his rejection...

Friends. Right. Apparently they were not only going to be friends, they were now going to be *awkward* friends.

Unless she went to find him, right now, and just blurted that out.

If the reason we're not going to have crazy hot sex is because it'll ruin our friendship, then we might as well have the crazy hot sex because frankly, the friendship appears to have been already ruined.

Ashley smiled at her reflection in the bathroom mirror as she washed her hands. Yeah, that would go over well. Assuming she could grow the large enough set of balls she'd need to actually say it.

She was still smiling—although a tad grimly—as she pushed open the bathroom door. But her smile faded fast because Bull and Todd were standing out in the hall, obviously waiting for her and blocking her path back to the mess—which was the only way to get to both the lounge and Dunk's office.

There was a door behind her that led outside to the parade grounds, but she was not going to run away into the darkness of the night. Not this time.

"Jig's up," Bull said, and Todd chimed in with, "We saw you."

She had no clue what they meant, so Bull added, "This afternoon…?"

But she was so focused on what *they'd* done—switching sides and "killing" her during the paintball game—that she still didn't understand, and she shook her head.

Until Todd spelled it out. "When you were kissing the SEAL…?"

Oh, God…

"That wasn't, um…" she started, unable to finish her sentence, because she still wasn't quite sure what that kiss was or wasn't, *and* it was none of their damn business.

"Um…" Bull mocked her. "You weren't just kissing, you were dry humping him. I'm sure you had fun tonight, during your extremely long *visit* to Sarasota."

Todd giggled.

Ashley sighed and shook her head at her incredible, almost impossibly bad luck.

"But that ended fast—he's already done with you," Bull pointed out. "Unless *you've* moved on. Hmmm…" He turned to his friend. "Maybe she's some kind of frog-hog."

"Well, obviously," Todd said. "Rosetti's next on her list."

"Slade, check." Bull laughed. "Rosetti, she's ready!"

Oh, dear, sweet God. Ashley had never heard the phrase *frog-hog* before, but it didn't take much imagination to figure out that it meant some kind of Navy SEAL groupie. Frog was a nickname for SEALs—because they'd started out in WWII as Navy Frogmen. Hog was… hog.

Nice.

And really, the unflattering name was just another form of slut-shaming. A man could be a super-model groupie and get high-fived for his "valiant efforts" to bed the entire cast of the current Victoria's Secret catalogue. He was called a *player* or a *playboy* or, frankly, just a normal *red-blooded* man. But when a woman did the exact same thing…? She was called terrible names, including *hog*.

Personally, the idea of sleeping with a long line of men simply because of one specific achievement, rather than their individual attractiveness and winning personalities was never going to be Ashley's thing. In fact, casual sex of any kind was not her thing—and maybe that was part of her problem. She believed that romance—and the sex that came with it—was some terribly serious life-or-death choice, instead of a far more lighthearted frolic filled with pleasure and sunshine and laughter.

God forbid she actually enjoy herself and have a little fun.

"Excuse me, please," Ashley said, working hard to keep her voice even as she tried to move past them. There was no point in having any kind of a conversation with these particular troglodytes. She wasn't going to convince them they were wrong, and it wasn't worth her time or effort.

But finding Jim and telling him that *no*, she really *didn't* want to be his awkward friend because she'd far prefer to see what would happen if she kissed him again…? That *was* worth both her time and her effort.

But the idiots blocking the hallway didn't budge. "One down," Bull smirked. "Four to go."

"Please move," Ashley said.

But Bull just laughed as he took a step closer, which made her take a step back. She'd never really thought of him as anything but a nuisance, but now she realized how big he was. And how badly lit the hallway was. And her back bumped the wall, but he kept coming. "Good luck, though, with the senior chief because he's—"

"Hey!" Thomas had come out of the lounge and was at the end of the hall. "Back the hell off!"

Bull and Todd both moved at that—fast—slipping around past Ashley and heading for the exit down at the end of the hall. "Relax, brah, no one's getting in your way," Bull called back to Thomas, "But heads up, she's a frog-hog—you might wanna be proactive with the course of antibiotics!"

The door slapped shut behind them, muffling their raucous laughter as they moved off into the night.

Thomas was just a shadowy shape at the end of the hall, but he came toward her. "You okay?"

Her heart was still pounding, but she nodded.

"What the *fuck* was that about?" Oh, good. Jim had come out of Dunk's office at the sound of Thomas's raised voice.

"Just Bull and Todd being Bull and Todd," Ashley said, adding as she swiftly went out into the mess, past Thomas, "I'm fine. Sorry about that."

But Jim wasn't willing to let it go—lurking there, an even bigger shadow in the dimly lit mess. "You're *sorry*...? Bull insulted you like that and *you're* sorry...?"

"They're idiots," Ashley told him as she drew close enough to see the anger on his face. "Do you mind if we go into Dunk's office, LT, to talk?"

"They're idiots," he repeated her again—standing there just as solidly unmovable as Bull and Todd had been. He was outraged and indignant, and—unlike her—unwilling to simply let it go. "But you just let them dis you and walk away."

"I didn't *let* them do anything," Ashley pointed out. "I can't control what they do—or think. I can only control my response."

"Which is what?" he asked. "To shrug it off...?"

She sighed. "Yes, you know what? *Yes.* For a lot of reasons that I know you can't possibly understand."

He made an exasperated noise.

So she kept going. "Come on, Jim. Do you really think my having a conversation with Bull and Todd would change anything?"

"Yeah, actually, I do," he said. "I think if you stood up to them, they would realize that they can't just walk all over you—disrespect you to your face. Where do *they* get off insulting you like that? Freaking *frog-hog*..."

"Well, for one thing," Ashley told him a tad more sharply than she'd intended, "they saw me kissing you."

"And *this* is where I grab Rio and go." Thomas, who'd been hovering, vanished back in the direction of the lounge as Jim swore.

"Yeah," Ashley agreed with his salty language as he took her by the arm and pulled her with him into the privacy of Dunk's office.

But he wasn't done arguing. "First of all, *I* kissed *you*," he said. "So, you *might* want to get that right, and you know, *maybe* get a little angry at *me*, too...?"

Ashley stared at him. "Why would I—"

"Because I fucking kissed you without thinking!"

"You already made that very clear," she countered.

"No, Jesus! God, I mean, yes, but I also didn't look around first," he shot back. "I didn't think *Hey, maybe I shouldn't fucking do this completely inappropriate thing because some douchebag lowlifes might be watching* and now they're fucking calling you nasty-ass names, and your response is *Oh, well...? Boys will be boys...?*"

"I did *not* say that."

"*Just Bull and Todd being Bull and Todd*," he quoted her. "Sounds equally defeatist to me. *Nothing's ever gonna change...*"

"I didn't say *that*, either."

"I'm paraphrasing," he said. "But you're right. Nothing's ever going to fucking change unless you do something to fucking change it."

"Why does it have to be me?" Ashley shot back. "Why don't *you* fucking change it?"

Jim smiled tightly. "Well, well, *there* she is."

"No, she is not," she countered. "And what does *that* mean, anyway? That letting myself react in anger—which, again—news-flash—changes nothing—is somehow more genuine than not...? That's just not true."

"I think you're afraid to get angry. Like, really melt-down, brain-boiling angry."

Ashley laughed her disgust. "And I think *you're* afraid of... quite possibly nearly every *other* emotion. Including—especially—intimacy."

"I didn't realize intimacy was an emotion," he said.

"You know what I meant," she said. "Anger is just a cover for fear. And you're terrified. And you know what? I am, too, but at least I admit it!" That verbal punch hit him hard—she could see it on his face as he flinched—and she immediately felt bad. "I'm sorry."

He swore again. "Don't apologize! You're always apologizing! And I'm the one who should be apologizing to you. I know how freaking hard this whole camp thing has been for you, and I made it worse by kissing you in front of a goddamned audience."

"Hello," she said. "I was there, too. So you can beat yourself up all you want, but hey, I wasn't exactly fighting you off."

"Because you *don't* fight! You don't let yourself get angry, and you don't fight! You just fucking surrender!"

He was right, it was true. In the car, she'd immediately surrendered, instead of arguing. Instead of saying, *This thing between us is pretty darn hot, and I hear you, but I'd really like to see where this could go...*

"You're right," she whispered now. "I give up far too quickly, don't I?"

"Hell, yeah," he said. And then he surprised her by running both hands down his face as he made a noise of both annoyance and frustration before admitting, "And you're right, too. I'm scared out of my mind!"

It was *that* look—the vulnerability—in his eyes that gave her the courage to do it. To take a step forward, and then another.

He saw her coming—she saw *that* in his eyes, too. And at first it was an expression of disbelief, and if that's all she'd seen she might've stopped herself. But then it turned to heat. It was a reflection of everything she was feeling—everything she wanted.

So she reached up and pulled his head down and she kissed him.

CHAPTER FOURTEEN

Jim knew that he shouldn't kiss her back.

He knew it, but he didn't let that stop him as he pulled Ashley hard against him, one hand wrapping around her waist and the other against the smoothness of her face, fingers tangling in the softness of her hair as he damn near inhaled her.

Because in the cosmic scheme of things, what did it matter? Why not have a moment or two of pleasure while he could…?

She seemed to want what he wanted, so… fuck it.

As they kissed and kissed and kissed and *kissed*, Jim thought—a few times—about her penchant to surrender. And he wondered—briefly—if this was that. The path of least resistance. Yeah, he could tell she was uncomfortable doing this here, in Dunk's outer office. But other than looking hard at the door to make sure it was locked after he'd backed them into it to latch it, she kinda wasn't hesitating.

True, she didn't exactly unfasten his shorts to stroke him. But when he pulled her with him onto the sofa so that she was straddling him, she definitely pressed even closer, rubbing herself against his length. And she voluntarily adiosed her shirt, pulling it swiftly over her head and tossing it onto what Jim would forever think of as the grandpa-chair—the one that wasn't as mushy as the others, and had solid arms so he could use his shoulders to help his less-than knees lift his body weight.

It was possible that, after they did this, whether it be make-out session or sex—he still wasn't sure whether or not she was going to stop them, but he knew damn well that she *should*—he was going to have to ask Ashley's help in pulling himself back up, off the soft couch.

And the shame of that added extra fuel to his fuck-it philosophy. His future was gonna be filled with pain of all kinds, but right now…? As Ashley made things more interesting by unfastening the front clasp of her bra…? Right now was pretty freaking awesome.

The marks she'd gotten from the paintball game were already mostly faded, but even with them, she was unbelievably perfect.

SEAL CAMP 121

Her breasts were soft and delicious, and his mouth and lips on her nipples—first one than the other as he kissed and licked and sucked and breathed in her sweet scent—made her gasp and softly moan.

But then she pulled back, and Jim braced himself for what had to be coming—a breathless confession that they'd gone too far but now sanity had intervened and they really had to stop.

Instead, she said, "I have to…" as she tried to unfasten both her jeans and his shorts.

To which he gallantly responded with, "I got mine," and made fast work with the button and zipper as she pushed herself off of him and did that distinctly female dance of shimmying out of her skinny jeans.

She wanted to be *more* naked, not less. Which was fine with the part of him that wanted to orgasm himself into oblivion in an attempt to stop feeling this hair-on-fire panic.

But the other part of him—the part that really, *really* liked her—controlled his vocal cords, so he opened his mouth and said, "In full disclosure, I just had a phone call with my CO. My *former* CO. I just got notified that… my days of active duty are over."

Ashley had finally managed to kick her feet free from her jeans, but now she froze—all blue eyes, golden hair, pink panties, and bare breasts.

"Oh, my God," she said. "Jim, I'm so sorry. I had no idea." She must've realized that she was nearly naked, because she hugged her jeans to her chest even as she came to sit beside him on that sofa, her concern nearly palpable. "If you'd rather talk about—"

He stopped *that* insanity by kissing her. And pulling her back onto his lap when she kissed him back.

Talk.

Right.

He was following the time-honored SEAL tradition of going commando, yet he hadn't freed himself from his pants—it had seemed presumptive.

But as Ashley kissed him—as he kissed her back and ran his hands over all that gorgeous, soft skin—she straddled him and pushed herself against him and he was well aware that there was only a slip of pink silk keeping him from doing something seriously stupid.

"Please tell me," she breathed between kisses, "you have a

condom."

He did. So he told her that he did, and she quickly shed her panties as he used it to cover himself, even as the stern or stupid part of him felt the need to say, "We shouldn't do this."

But she just kissed him again, her hands around him, stroking him, guiding him...

And then, God, he was inside of her.

Ashley pushed Jim deeply inside of her as she heard herself cry out.

This was better than the A-plus-plus fantasies that she'd imagined. The way he was looking at her, the way that he kissed her, held her, moved both with and against her...

She honestly hadn't known that making love could feel this perfect—this all-consuming and complete. And she'd had plenty of great sex in her life with which to compare.

But Ashley could see more than fire in Jim's eyes—she glimpsed the fear and hurt of his still-raw loss beneath his desire and need—and she knew that she was seeing it only because he was letting her in. She was seeing a soul that he'd bared for her alone.

She tried, through touching him, kissing him, making love to him, to tell him that everything was going to be okay—that she'd help him, gladly, as he transitioned into the next phase of his life. That he was going to do something amazing and important and satisfying. That moving into the unknown didn't have to be scary— it could be exhilarating, and bring him great joy.

A lot like the joy she was feeling right now.

This man—this amazing, smart, funny, thoughtful, intelligent, caring, imperfect, complicated human being—was the man that Ash been waiting for, all her life.

And she came undone even as she held his gaze; until she had to give in and close her eyes because it was just too much to let him see into *her* soul, to let him see all she was feeling as she unraveled.

But her chagrin at coming too quickly—she wanted to do exactly this for hours and hours and *hours*—was tempered by the fact that he then came quickly, too. Bucking beneath her as he groaned, "Ashley..."

The sound of her name ripped from him like that was everything she'd ever wanted, and she kissed him again and again and again.

And then there they were. She could feel his heart still pounding as fast and as hard as hers as he held on to her as tightly as she clung to him.

"Jesus," he breathed into her ear.

She laughed softly.

But then he said it again. "Jesus, what have I done…?"

And Ashley stopped laughing as she pulled back to look at him.

CHAPTER FIFTEEN

"What have *you* done?" Ashley asked. "You do know that *we* did this…? I mean, this was definitely a *we*."

As Jim looked at the gorgeous naked woman whose soft, warm body still surrounded him, he knew the truth. He wanted this. He wanted her. He wanted more. And most of all, he wanted it to be real.

But he was going to mess it up—how could he not, considering the high stress and flat-out bitter unhappiness he was facing. Hey, what a brilliant idea! Simultaneously learn how to *not* be a SEAL *and* make a relationship work for the very first time in his life.

He was going to decimate her, except no, he, too, would be road-kill when this dust finally settled. He was going to decimate them both.

And the idea of that much failure, all at the same time, was too much.

"Ashley, I can't do this," he admitted. "Except, we already did. I should've stopped before we… Shit, I'm so sorry, this is entirely my fault."

"No, it's not. That's just… not… No." She was clearly shocked at his words, and even shaken by what must've felt to her like a complete 180 turn-around. Yet she still somehow managed to be concerned for him as she climbed off of him and quickly pulled on her clothes.

How could she not be angry? It was mind-blowing as Jim made equally quick work of the condom then he, too, adjusted his shorts and zipped. And he felt a hot rush of anger himself—at the world, at himself, and even at her. "Can I be… brutally honest with you?"

"Please," she said as she pulled on her shirt and sat on the very edge of the sofa—close but not too close. "I'd very much like to talk about this, because… also to be honest, I really don't understand what the problem is. I mean, I know you're upset—and you have every right to be—by the news about—"

"I screwed up by letting this happen," he said, knowing that she would notice his word choice.

And she did. "You didn't want... You *let it* happen...?" But then she went too far. "Oh, my God, but... you did consent, right...? Please tell me I didn't miss the part where you said *no*..."

"No!" Jim said. "Jesus! I mean, yes, I mean, it was completely consensual! It was just really, *really* stupid. I'm your instructor and I just fucked you in Dunk's office, and that's not okay."

She flinched at his brutally inelegant description of what they'd just done. But she still said, "I can assure you that I wasn't thinking of you as my instructor when we—"

He cut her off. "That's not how it works, and you know it."

She nodded, but then shook her head. "I get that, but I very much wanted this. I'm the one who kissed you first, out in the mess hall."

"No, *I'm* the one who kissed you first—earlier this afternoon and it was..." Jim couldn't finish because it wasn't quite true. He'd kissed her out by their trailers because he'd temporarily lost his mind. But now, he took a deep breath, and told her, "I like you, I do. I think you're amazing. You know that."

"Oh, God," she said, because she was clearly familiar with the coded subtext that reinforced what he'd already told her—about wanting to be her friend.

It both was and wasn't a lie, and Jim clung to the shreds of his very real desire not to hurt her—or rather to hurt her quickly now, when it would only briefly sting instead of break her heart.

"I've been... actively trying to, um, make you snap. Piss you off." Also not a lie, despite having nothing to do with what just happened here. "All that... excessive touching on the paintball field...? That was part of my strategy. To come on too strong and push you into fighting back. Only you didn't. Fight. And suddenly it all... went too far."

Except the way that she was looking at him now—as her shocked confusion turn to horrified disbelief—made his own heart break. Because this wasn't just a small, sharp sting. She looked as if he'd just stabbed her in the heart.

But he was a SEAL, and he'd learned the importance of never leaving a targeted threat half-dead, so he administered the emotional double-pop needed to make her walk away from him and not look back.

"I even talked to Dunk about it—about you," he admitted, and now embarrassment mixed with the disbelief that was swimming in her eyes. "About the best way to push you into getting angry—he disagreed with me, by the way, and ordered me to stop. But I didn't. I thought if I did what Bull and Todd did, that you'd, you know, unleash your rage *on me*, and you'd see that it's okay for you to get angry."

"So this was... some kind of a... twisted SEAL World exercise?" She laughed as she stood up, but it was part sob. "A lesson...? How was it supposed to go? What was I supposed to do to get an A? Slap you across the face and say *Unhand me, sir!* Like that has *anything* to do with real life...?"

Jim nodded. "Good. Get mad. You should be mad. And yes. I thought you would stop me—us. Stop this from happening. And when you didn't...? Well, I know that you know..." He forced a shrug and a laugh, and torched the remains of their relationship. "*Boys will be boys.*"

Ashley's eyes widened. But she didn't get loud. She didn't scream *Fuck you* at him, as he completely deserved. Instead, she got quiet and still—her eyes enormous in her face as tears brimmed. And when she spoke it was in a whisper. "Wow, I really failed your life lesson, Instructor. Worst of all, I failed mine. I just keep making the same idiotic mistake. God, I'm a fool. I actually thought you were... But no, you're Brad two-point-oh. New and improved and extra shitty." She wiped her eyes and her nose and sniffed and it was as if she'd hit her own reset button, because she was instantly more composed. "I would prefer it if what happened in here—the instructor-fucking—stays in here, but... it really doesn't matter who you tell. I'm leaving in the morning. I'm done."

And now it was Jim who was getting angry—because she wasn't. "Oh, perfect! *I* screw up, and *you* run away—you quit. That's great. That's definitely what should happen here. Instead of, you know, *me* leaving."

She unlocked the door, opened it. "I'm not running, and I'm certainly not quitting. I'm leaving because I'm graduating. Lesson learned—ironic, huh? You really are quite the skilled teacher." But then she paused and looked at him, and whispered. "*Boys will be boys* because of the toxic things we teach them, but... I mistook you for a man. Maybe someday you'll finally grow up, Lieutenant, because until you do, you're not going to find whatever it is that you're looking for. And I hope someday you grow up and find it—I really do."

And with that she left the room, closing the door silently but tightly behind her.

Jim sat there, forcing himself not to go after her—to apologize, to grovel and confess that he was lying, but he knew...

She'd be better off without him—non-SEAL-him, adrift and so fucking angry, and yes, toxic. She got that word right.

Although, maybe in a few years... Yeah, right. He shut that shit down. Who was he kidding? Her face and eyes, right before she'd left this room... He'd burned this bridge completely. Full flame-thrower. Also...? There was no way a woman as fantastic as Ashley wouldn't be married with one-and-a-half kids in a few years, if and when he was finally ready. Assuming, that is, he survived not being a SEAL.

No, she would definitely find someone who deserved her. Who would appreciate her and cherish her and love her, endlessly...

And no way was he crying. He used Ashley's reset. A swipe of his eyes and nose. A deep breath.

Fine. He was fine.

But, shit, he had to text Chief Taylor with the sign-in info for the account he'd created for the security cam app that they'd set up with those cameras both outside and in Ashley's condo. Double-shit, because if she was really leaving camp, she'd be walking back, directly into that nightmare. He checked his phone one last time, looking at the glimpse of her life, both outside of her front door and inside her living room, before he signed out of the app for the last time.

And by the time he finally locked Dunk's office door, and limped his sorry ass all the way back to his trailer, Ashley's lights were off.

He'd get up early and talk to Dunk, because *he* was the one who had to leave. He'd promised the senior chief that he wouldn't quit, but it wouldn't take much explaining to get himself fired. And enough campers had quit that it wouldn't take much shuffling to rearrange the remaining people into workable teams—including Ashley who absolutely should stay.

Still, he stood there, in the dark, wishing he could time travel—to just a few years ago. He'd find Ashley, pre-Brad—he still didn't know what Brad had done, although her calling him Brad two-point-oh had stung.

But he'd step out of his time machine and he'd still be a SEAL, with two good knees and many years in the Teams ahead of him.

Although, even as he imagined finding Ash and sweeping her off her feet, he realized he probably would've screwed it up because, back then, he wasn't even close to ready for a woman as amazing as she was.

And in that moment of despair, he almost did it. He almost limped over to Ashley's trailer and pounded on the door, to apologize, to explain, to beg her not to hate him.

But Jim knew that tonight's panic about the future was nothing compared to what was coming at him tomorrow. The bullshit of paperwork and the printed acknowledgement that he was finally done. He'd have to tell his teammates, his family. His mother would see his retirement only as a good thing, which would hurt, because she wouldn't understand the impact of his loss.

His teammates would, but there was no way Jim would talk to any of them about it—make them face the harsh reality of their own steadily approaching use-by dates...?

No.

He was going to have to work through this on his own.

Jim stood there in the humid darkness of the night, feeling more alone than he'd ever felt in his entire life, with a solid sense of dread that, instead of "fixing" a "mistake," he may have just fucked up his life beyond all hope.

He finally went into his trailer, limping painfully up the steps, going inside, and shutting the door.

Ashley had cried.

And then she'd packed.

And then she'd left, turning off the light in her trailer and locking the door behind her before heading back to the mess, where she waited in the darkness for her Lyft to come and pick her up.

Jim's alarm went off just before dawn, as the rising sun made the sky glow.

He didn't bother to shower, since he'd done that in the middle of the night. He'd gotten out of bed to do it—Ashley's scent had been haunting him, and keeping him from falling asleep.

Not that showering had helped.

But it was finally morning—and a nice, fresh, cool, clear one, too. As he hobbled his way out of his trailer, he expected to see Ashley's windows open wide as she packed her suitcase, making good on her promise to leave.

But the trailer was locked up tight—dark and silent.

Damnit, how had he missed her...? Apparently, as early as he'd gotten up, Ashley had gotten up earlier.

Jim's knees were stiff and he had a hell of a bad headache—coffee would help. He hurried down the trail as quickly as he could, but halfway to the mess, he ran into Clark, who was heading for the trailers.

"Hey, LT," he said.

"Hey, how's Kenneth?" Jim asked.

"*So* much better," Clark said. "If he continues to improve, he's getting released from the hospital tonight. I'm here to pack up our gear. Chief Duncan says he's doing something called *rolling us for medical reasons*—so we can both come back, together, for free, for another camp session after Kenneth's better—probably some time this summer. Right now, Kenneth's mom and dad are renting a beach house out on Siesta Key for a coupla weeks, so he can recuperate for the rest of spring break. They've, um, invited me to stay, so..."

"Kenneth's sister Louise gonna be there, too?" Jim asked.

Clark winced. "Busted, but yeah."

"She's completely out of your league," Jim told the kid.

"I'm well aware."

"Don't let that stop you," Jim said. "I'm giving you seven years to marry her in your dress whites with your SEAL Budweiser pinned to your chest. Do it in fewer, and make me proud."

Clark laughed, but then surprised Jim with a hug. "You're the only person—besides Ashley—who thinks of me as more than, you know, a random bag of dicks."

"You're also a random bag of dicks," Jim said. "But that's what makes you special."

Clark laughed. "Thanks, sir."

"You, um, driving Ashley back with you, into Sarasota...?" He tried to make his question sound casual. Talk about a bag of dicks...

"No, she's already up in Tampa," the kid said. "At the airport. She emailed me, like an hour ago, to check on Kenneth. I was already awake—I kinda never went to sleep—so I called her and she told me things had blown up at work. She has to get back to California, ASAP. She couldn't get a flight out of Sarasota, so she's on, I think it's the 6:45 flight, stopping in... I wanna say, Atlanta?"

"6:45...?" Jim looked at his watch in dismay. It was already oh-six-hundred, and Tampa was nearly two hours north.

"Yeah, but no. She just texted me—her flight's been delayed, something like six hours. I think she's already at the airport bar. She mentioned having a glass of wine for breakfast, and I'm not sure she was kidding."

"I'm sorry I missed her." Understatement of the century.

"Yeah, I'm kinda surprised you didn't drive her to the airport. I thought you guys were—"

Jim stopped him. "No." He forced a smile, because Clark was looking at him hard.

The kid wasn't fooled. "She's outa your league, too, but... She liked you. I don't know what you were waiting for. She hasn't gotten even remotely near anyone since Brad screwed her over."

You're Brad two-point-oh...

"What exactly did Brad do, or not do...?" Jim asked. "She mentioned him, but I didn't get details."

"Our father hired him to marry her," Clark said.

"I'm sorry, *what...*?"

"Yeah, it's as bad as it sounds. Brad's a lawyer, he applied for an associate position at Dad's firm, Dad interviewed him and thought, *Huh.* And he made Brad a deal. If Brad could get Ash to the altar, Dad would make him a partner—no pay-in, just *boom.* And if he could talk her into working there, too, he'd get a corner office. So Bradley went a'courtin'. He almost did it, too. They were engaged for... I don't even know how many months."

"Jesus..."

"Ash only found out because Brad told her. Confession time. It was weeks before the wedding, but Brad shows up, knocking on her door, weeping. Like, *Baby, I know this sounds bad and it started out as this awful, mercenary thing, and I'm so ashamed, but then I met you and I fell in love... blah blah blah.* She was wrecked." Clark looked at him. "Like, how could she believe him? I mean, was this part of the con? Confess this now, because God forbid she finds out in ten years, right…? Long story short, she dumped him and didn't look back. But she hasn't exactly looked forward, either. At least not until she met you."

Fuck.

Fuck.

Jim had thought that giving Ashley that bullshit story—*I was trying to make you angry but went too far*—would be easier and less painful than the truth: *I want you so badly, but I'm too scared.*

And yeah, it had been easier and less painful—for him.

She had been left believing—again—that she hadn't truly been desired.

And Jim simply could not let that stand.

He had to get to Tampa. To the airport. Now. "Can I catch a ride with you, into Sarasota?" he asked Clark.

"If you can be ready to leave in about twenty minutes, sure."

"Kid, I've seen the inside of your trailer. You're seriously gonna pack all that shit in twenty minutes…?"

Clark smiled. "With all due respect, LT, I'll be done in ten. I was giving you a little extra time."

"You were born to be a SEAL," Jim told him. "I'll be ready when you are."

As Clark headed for his RV, Jim set off at a knee-wrenching jog down the trail. He needed coffee—and a quick but sure-to-be-loud conversation with Dunk.

Ashley sat at the gate in the airport, trying desperately to read. She had a mountain of great, unread books on her e-reading app, but nothing caught her attention, and she flipped aimlessly from one to the next.

This was where, if her life were a rom-com movie, Jim would come running into the airport, searching for her, shouting her name. And then, as she stood, he'd spot her and rush up to her, then drop to his knees to beg her to forgive him, to confess his undying love, and possibly even to ask for her hand in marriage.

Except there was no way he'd be able to drop to his poor, battered knees—and right, *that* was the reason her insane little fantasy was never going to happen.

And even if it did… The sad truth was that she no longer wanted him. Just like Brad before him, there was literally nothing Jim could say or do to make up for the appallingly awful way he'd treated her.

Ashley sat with that for a while, wondering if it was really true, or if it was just something she was telling herself—and trying hard to believe in—so that she didn't fall apart.

She spent some time Googling therapists in the San Felipe area. She knew of some—women who specialized in helping other women out of abusive relationships by working on reinforcing self-worth and self-esteem. Because there was a pattern. Women who struggled to value their own selves often wound up in relationships with manipulators, over and over again. Predatory and abusive men recognized and targeted the vulnerable. And while that was not the women's fault, the pattern *could* be broken by women learning to love themselves—to recognize that they deserved to be treated with real love and respect.

And although Ashley hoped that she'd never tolerate a relationship with a man who was physically or even verbally abusive, there was certainly a pattern to her behavior. She was attracted to men who were assholes and users—there was no denying that fact.

God, it was embarrassing to remember how quick she'd been last night, to assume what she was feeling was love. A little dick—well, a rather large one—after having gone without sex for too long, and she was ready and eager to give her heart away to a man she barely knew.

Barely? She didn't know him *at all*. God, she'd only met the man a few days ago. She'd made stupid assumptions, and created a persona for him that was kind, and caring, and funny, and smart, and imperfectly perfect for her... Oh God, don't let her cry...

Ashley stashed her iPad in her purse, and stood as she raised the pull-handle on her rolling carry-on bag, heading for the privacy of the closest ladies' room. Again.

Jim walked into a full staff meeting in Dunk's outer office—where just last night he and Ash had...

Everyone looked up as he came through the door, which didn't help him feel any less self-conscious.

"Hey," Dunk greeted him. "Didn't expect to see you until later. I figured you'd be driving Ashley to the airport in Tampa. I got a note from her that she had to get back to California in a hurry, and I thought—"

"No," Jim said. "She, uh, must've, um, gotten a car."

Dunk wasn't even remotely fooled, and his eyes narrowed. "I heard about Bull and Todd's bullshit out on the paintball field, and today they'll be emptying black tanks under my supervision. Tomorrow they'll have a choice between an all-day sensitivity training session, or leaving and not coming back until they take the damn class, and I'm banking on them choosing the latter. But I'm guessing they're not why Ashley left."

"No," Jim agreed.

"What the fuck did you do?" Dunk asked.

Jim looked around the room at the faces of his teammates. Lucky, as always, was perpetually amused, and he looked back and forth from Dunk to Jim as if he couldn't wait to see what was going to happen next. Rio's eyebrows were raised, and Thomas grimly shook his head as he stared down at his feet, as if he already knew the answer and was embarrassed for Jim in advance.

"I fucked up," Jim admitted. "Badly. I'm actually here for you to fire me, so I can go to the airport in Tampa and find Ashley and…"

"You'll have to buy a ticket to get to the gate," Rio said.

Jim held up his phone. "Already done. Same flight."

Dunk was disgusted. "That's definitely not a good idea. To harass her at the airport—"

"I won't harass her," Jim promised. "I just need to talk to her—"

"Said every man, everywhere, who ever had a restraining order taken out on him," Thomas pointed out.

"I got the news last night that I'm out of the Teams," Jim told his friends. "Medical's not gonna try to fix my knees anymore. It's over."

"Ah, shit," Dunk breathed. "Jim, I'm so sorry."

"And I know that's not an excuse for what I said to Ashley," Jim said, "but… Dunk, please, you gotta fire me. I promised you I wouldn't quit, but I made her believe that I didn't care about her, at all, and that's such a fucking lie, because, God, I'm in love with her…"

His voice broke and he knew that he sounded insane—to his own ears as well. But as those words left his lips, he realized it was true. This feeling of wanting, of sorrow, of motherfucking *agony* from knowing just how badly he'd hurt her...

"I swear to you," Jim promised the senior chief through eyes that—Christ!—suddenly swam with tears, "I just want to tell her that I lied. I honestly don't expect it to change anything, not for me, but maybe it will for her, because I know her, and she's... hating herself right now. If she tells me to get lost—*when* she tells me that—I won't push. I promise you, I'll back away."

Dunk sighed. "You can't call her? Talk on the phone?"

"I tried," Jim said. He'd added Ashley's cell to his phone's list of contact while they were at the hospital—in case the doctor came out to talk to them while she'd been searching the vending machines for food. "She didn't pick up."

Dunk sighed again.

"Ah, come on, Senior," Lucky said. "Give the man a chance."

Dunk looked at Jim. "I do this? You owe me."

Jim nodded. "You know that I already do."

"You're fired," Dunk said. "Asshole."

And Jim ran, out of the mess and back to his trailer to pack his bag.

Ashley left the ladies' room, pulling her carry-on bag behind her.

Her running shoes were silent on the tile floor—it was strange but liberating to travel without heels and she'd probably never travel in anything but sneakers and jeans again. But the wheels of her bag clicked and clattered in a reassuring cadence along the now-familiar path back to the gate.

"Ashley."

Someone stepped in front of her, and she stopped short, looking up at...

Jim.

He was carrying a duffel bag and wearing the same clothes he'd had on last night—before he'd taken them off to... how had he put it? *Fuck her in Dunk's office.* His brown hair was a charming mess and the stubble on his chin was GQ-photo-shoot worthy.

Fucking men. They could roll out of bed looking sexy and per-fect, and she hated him for that, even as her stupid heart leaped. It actually leaped and danced in her chest because he'd followed her here. What kind of fool was she...?

"Please," he said, as a crowd of harried travelers streamed around them on both sides. "Can we talk…?"

"No," she told him even as she made the mistake of looking into his eyes.

He was chagrined and apologetic—and she saw it again. That same fear and vulnerability he'd let her glimpse last night.

Which was just part of his pathetic act.

"Excuse me." She tried to navigate her way around him.

"Ashley, I'm so sorry. I got scared, and, well, the truth is, I lied about… almost everything, and I'd really like to explain."

She stopped. Turned to face him. "Is that so I'll feel better, or you'll feel better…? Because I'm getting a heavy whiff, here, of *you* wanting to feel better, and I'm not sure I'm in the mood for that."

"You have every right to be angry," Jim said. "Can we just… step out of the traffic—"

"No," she said. "And I'm not angry. You still haven't made me angry. At least not at you. I'm a *little* angry at myself, for being so quick to believe that you're someone you're not. But that's not on you, that's on me. You can't help being a piece of shit."

Jim winced. "Ouch."

"Oh, no, excuse me," she said. "A *lying* piece of shit, because you just admitted that you lied—I'm not sure about what, except apparently now I'm supposed to believe whatever it is that you *now* want to tell me, except you've just told me you're a liar…? How do I know you're not simply lying again?"

"Jesus, you're magnificent when you're angry."

"I'm *not*—"

"Ashley, I was actively trying to push you away when I said what I said last night."

"Good job," she said. "You succeeded."

"I kissed you because I wanted to," he told her, glancing around at the curious onlookers streaming past them, and lowering his voice to add, "What happened in Dunk's office also happened, absolutely, because I wanted it, not because I was playing some… stupid game. That was just bullshit. I lied about *that*. I wanted you. I still do, God help me. But then, after we… I… I panicked." He had tears in his eyes. "I'm not a SEAL anymore, at least I won't be in a very short amount of time. And all I could think was, *Why would you want me…? And I don't think I can do this, start this… amazing and terrifying thing with you, because it's all just so freaking hard…"*

"God, you're an idiot," Ashley said. "Or maybe you think I am. You're either a manipulative asshole, a lying asshole, or an idiotic asshole. So, as tempting as it is to consider welcoming you back into my life, I'm gonna pass."

Jim nodded. Wiped his eyes. Sniffed. Managed a weak smile. "That's, um, a really good decision. I understand. Completely. I just, um, wanted to make sure you knew that the screw-up here isn't you—it's me. And that I'm so sorry I hurt you by making you believe that... I don't love you. Because... I do."

Ashley stood there, looking at him. "You love me. Of course you do. Right on time."

She didn't believe him. She didn't forgive him. She wasn't sure she ever would. And he was right about the fact that he was the screw-up here. But she was also at fault. For falling for yet another asshole, and attempting to find a comfortable place for herself in his we-are-not-equal world.

And Ashley realized in a flash of clarity that was so sharp, its edges nearly cut her to the quick: *She didn't need to change.* Not radically, the way she'd thought she had to change when she'd signed up for the camp. Yes, she should and she certainly *could* not only stop dating assholes, and also be more assertive in her personal life—more *in command.* She'd learned both that word and the feeling that came with it during her short camp session, and that was a good thing. A useful tool.

But to try to change herself more drastically to... what? To become more like a man...?

No. *She*—and the over fifty percent of the world's population who were women and girls—didn't need to change.

The rest of the world did.

"Good luck, Lieutenant," she said, and this time, when she turned, he let her walk away.

Jim—the Lieutenant—was on her flight.

So not only did Ashley have to sit near him at the gate in Tampa, she had to sit near him for the layover at the gate in Atlanta, too.

He was, thank God for small favors, completely respectful. But she was aware of him.

She was aware that his knees were hurting. On the flight to

Atlanta—a relatively short hop from Tampa—he'd somehow squeezed himself into the dread middle seat in coach, several rows up from her. He'd spent much of the time on his feet, in the aisle, which was probably only marginally less painful than sitting without proper legroom.

On the flight to San Diego, she had an aisle seat and she was ready to trade with him, but the flight wasn't full, and all it took was a quiet word to the flight attendant: "The very tall man in row 18 is an active duty Navy SEAL, dealing with a knee injury. Is there anyway you could move him into first class, so he'll be more comfortable?"

As the flight attendant approached him and moved him up to the front of the plane, he glanced back at Ashley, well aware of what she'd done.

In fact, he sent her a drink—a plastic cup of red wine.

She drank it with the sandwich she'd picked up at the kiosk in Atlanta, then closed her eyes and tried to sleep.

At the gate in San Diego, Jim waited for Ashley to get off the plane.

She looked neither happy nor surprised to see him standing there.

"Thanks," he said. "For, you know…"

"You really need to learn to stand up for yourself," she told him, half tongue-in-cheek. "People want to help. Like, right now. You could ask for a wheelchair."

"Yeah, that's not gonna happen," he said.

She nodded. "Right. Well." She looked around as if to get her bearings.

"Baggage claim is this way," he said, leading her in that direction.

"I didn't check a bag," she said.

"Ground transportation's in the same place."

"Ah, yes," she said. "I made arrangements for a car…"

God, this was awkward.

She cleared her throat. "I'd offer to give you a lift, but Coronado's in the opposite direction from San Felipe."

"You're going home?" He asked it as a question, and she looked at him like the idiot that he was.

"Yes, because... I live there...?"

"Right. Of course. I just... should've told Taylor and Skelly to change the locks," Jim said. "Your intruder's still at large."

Ashley stopped. "You're not responsible for me," she said. "You never were, and you certainly never will be."

Jim nodded, setting his duffel down at his feet. "I get that. I just... I care. About you. Your safety is important to me."

"Really?" she said. "You want me to be safe. Said the man who tried to goad me into getting angry, who accused me of, I don't know what—being weak because I chose not to throw down with Bull and Todd, when I was *alone* with them in a dark hallway, in the middle of the night...? What the hell do you think I was doing? I was making damn sure that I stayed safe! What planet do you come from, that you think my getting angry with men like Bull and Todd would do anything other than make me very, *very* unsafe? Together, they're three times my weight! How do you live to be as old as you are and not know what most women have learned by the time they're ten years old: That there's potential danger in any—*any*—disagreement with a man. So we de-escalate. By default. As quickly as we possibly can. *To stay safe!* You know, I came out of the bathroom and Bull and Todd were standing there, using their very large bodies to trap me in the hall. And you seriously thought I should've *shouted* at them for disrespecting me? I'm sorry, but *no*. I'm going to do what I did. I'm going to be polite. I'm going to use the only weapon I have *to stay safe*—words and logic and the norms of society—although those so-called social norms have decayed drastically over the past year and a half, thanks to the motherfucking pussy-grabber-in-chief!"

"God, I really do love it when you're angry." It was not the right thing to say—not by a mile—but he couldn't stop himself, because it was true.

"Fuck you, Lieutenant! Because you look at me and you think I'm never angry, but you are so wrong. If you want to know the truth—if that word means *anything* to you, lying liar that you are—I'm always—*always*—a little bit afraid. And *that* means I'm also always angry. It's hard not to be. I just don't have the luxury, like you do, of showing it!"

"Excuse me, ma'am, is everything okay over here?"

The airport security guard was a woman, and she was looking at Jim as if she was sizing up the fastest way to take him down. Her dark brown eyes lingered on his knee braces, and he knew that wasn't by accident. Her message was clear: *If you think your knees hurt now, wait'll you wrangle with me.*

"Everything's fine," he said, but she ignored him, instead waiting for Ashley to answer.

"My friend is an asshole," she told the guard as her own eyes filled with tears. "But I know he'd never hurt me—not that way, not physically." She turned to Jim even as her tears escaped down her cheeks. "Oh, the irony of finally finding a man I can be honest with, to unleash myself like that and truly *not* be afraid..."

"Ash, I'm sorry," he whispered. "I'm so sorry. Please—"

He reached for her, but she stepped back, and the guard stepped forward.

"I have to go," Ashley said. "Don't follow me, Jim. I really don't want to see you again. Not just tonight, not... ever."

She hurried away from him then, the wheels of her bag clattering on the airport floor.

Jim must've made a move—purely involuntary, total SEAL brain-stem, *gotta follow, gotta fix, gotta have, gotta win...* But the guard stepped in front of him. "Sir, I'm gonna have to ask you to wait. Just for a few minutes."

"I am, I will, I'm... sorry. And thanks. Really. For making sure she was safe." Because that's why the guard had stopped. She'd seen Ashley getting angry at Jim, and recognized, just as Ashley had said, that doing so might put her in danger.

The woman nodded, and then dug in her pockets and handed him a little packet of tissues. "Keep 'em," she said, and walked away.

It was only then Jim realized that he was crying, too.

CHAPTER SIXTEEN

Jim picked up his truck from the lot on base, and headed out to grab a burger and a beer for his second dinner.

He was exhausted—it was barely 1830, but that was 2130 in Florida, and he'd been on Eastern Time long enough to feel it. He also hadn't gotten much sleep last night. Still, he knew the best way to combat jetlag was to move as quickly as possible into the biorhythms of the new time zone, so instead of driving home and crashing into his bed, he was gonna eat another meal and force himself to stay awake, at least until the sun was fully down.

He wasn't up to socializing with any SEAL teammates, so he headed back over the bridge to his favorite mom and pop place called Werewulf's. He'd just sat down at the bar and caught the owner's eye—a woman named Greykell Perks who tended bar while her three kids cooked—when his phone buzzed with an incoming text.

Meals-at-the-bar at Werewulf's weren't meant to be eaten while staring at your phone. No, the burger experience came with sci-fi movie gems playing on the bar TV—tonight was *Escape from New York*, which deserved his full attention. Still, he pulled his phone partly out of his pocket just to see who he was going to ignore. He was betting it was Thomas King, checking in on him.

But the name on his phone's screen was *Ashley*, and Jim's heart actually pounded with hope as he broke his rule and took his phone out to read her text.

But then her words make his heart pound for completely different reason as he read them: *Sweetie, sorry to cancel last minute, can't do dinner tonight, must reschedule, maybe tomorrow?*

Sweetie? Jesus… He looked at his watch and did the math. Her trip to San Felipe from the airport would've brought her home to her condo right about…

Now.

This was an SOS message if he'd ever seen one.

It didn't take much to imagine what had happened. She'd gotten home, and whoever had broken in was there, waiting for her. She'd given her attacker some made up some story about her "boyfriend" coming over for dinner, and having to send him a text to cancel—in hopes that upon reading that text, Jim wou!d realize that something was *very* wrong.

"What can I get you, Jim?" Greykell asked, but Jim was already on his feet and heading for the door.

"Sorry, Grey, gotta run."

As he fast-walked, he searched his phone for the security app that was attached to the hidden cameras that Bobby Taylor and Wes Skelly had installed at Ashley's condo. He'd signed out last night, and when he tried to sign in now, the password failed. Of course it did. A stickler for internet security, the first thing Chief Taylor would do was change the password.

So now Jim full-on ran for his truck on knees that burned, threw himself inside and started the engine with a roar. Fastest way to San Felipe would be via back roads at this time of evening, so he headed roughly north and east as fast he could, even as he called Taylor through his Bluetooth.

The Chief picked up on the first ring, cheerful as always. "Hey, LT. You're on speaker! I'm in the car with Colleen. Rumor has it you came back early."

"Chief, I need Ashley DeWitt's home address."

"Uhhh…"

Colleen's voice came in. "Hi, Jim, how are you?"

"Kinda desperately needing Ashley's address. She just t—"

"She sent me an email this morning," Colleen spoke over him. "She didn't say what happened, other than that *some*thing happened with you, and that it was over. I'm sorry to hear that."

Bobby cut in. "With all due respect, sir, I'm gonna ask you to get that address directly from Ashley…? I mean, if she wants you to have it—"

"She just texted me," Jim said. "She's in trouble. Bob, I need you to check the security feed. She called me *sweetie*, and said she had to cancel plans for dinner tonight—"

"Hang on, I'm pulling into a parking lot so I can check the app," Bobby said, even as Colleen misunderstood.

"Jim," she said, "whatever plans you had with her, it's not… well, if I'm reading that email right, it's likely that she never intended to meet you in the first place."

"We didn't have plans for dinner," Jim said as clearly as he could. "She told me she didn't want to see me anymore. She made it very clear. That's what I'm trying to tell you, because suddenly I get a text where she's canceling the dinner that we weren't going to have unless pigs started flying..."

Bobby swore pungently. "You're right, LT. Recorded video footage shows her being accosted outside of her front door by a man with a handgun."

Jim drove faster. "I need her address."

"Oh, my God," Colleen said, "let me see..."

"Interior camera currently shows..." Bobby said. "Yeah, she's okay, I don't think he hurt her, but he's in her condo with her. She's put some distance between them, she's a few feet away from him now. She appears to be talking to him, doing something on her computer as he looks over her shoulder. He's got..." He swore again. "It's a Glock, LT. Nine millimeter."

Colleen rattled off an address that Jim quickly input into his GPS. "I'm ten minutes away," he reported.

"We're about twenty," Bobby said. "Wait for us, Jim! Colleen, call Wes. And Senior Chief Becker."

"I'm on it," she said.

"Colleen," Jim asked, his heart in his throat. "The gunman. Is it Brad?"

"No," she told him. "I don't know who it is, but it's definitely not Brad."

Greg Ramsey wanted to know where the hell Betsy, his soon-to-be ex-wife, was.

It was funny—not funny-ha-ha but a *little* bit interesting-funny—at first, anyway, because Ashley honestly couldn't place him as he came stomping down the outdoor corridor as she was attempting to unlock the front door to her condo.

She knew she'd seen him before, but she simply couldn't remember from where. And then it stopped being any kind of funny when he brandished that deadly looking gun and demanded that she tell him where Betsy was hiding.

And everything clicked into place.

The break-in. The search of her apartment—including the pockets of her clothes. Greg had been looking for information, for files, for records, for hand-scribbled notes, for anything that would tell him his soon-to-be ex-wife's whereabouts.

"I honestly don't know where Betsy is," Ash had said, and Greg had shoved that gun up right beneath her chin, slamming her head and shoulders against the wall beside her front door. She hit so hard that she saw stars.

"She's in a shelter," Ashley said quickly, aware that one jerk of his finger on the trigger would end her life. God, she didn't want to die. "I honestly don't know which one, but just give me a chance, and I can find out."

That wasn't really a lie. She could find out. She probably even would find out. But there was no way in hell she was going to let this man get anywhere near the woman he'd already spent years abusing. She'd die first.

But as he roughly grabbed her keys from her hands, unlocking the door and pushing her and her bag inside, she looked up toward where she knew those cameras had been recently installed.

Was anyone watching? She honestly didn't know. And no way was she simply going to passively wait to find that out.

Instead, as Greg had dug into her handbag to take possession of her phone so she couldn't call 9-1-1, she'd told him, "I'll need my computer to access the file. But first, you need to know that I made plans to meet Jim, my Navy SEAL boyfriend, here for dinner. At 7:30. If I don't text him, to tell him that something's come up, he's going to knock on that door. And when I don't answer, he's going to kick it down, and you'll probably kill him, but not before he kills you, too, so please let's *not* do that."

Greg had backed away and set down his gun—he was not as comfortable holding it as he pretended to be—as he looked at Ashley's phone. She gave him the code to unlock it, and spelled out *Slade* as she prayed he wouldn't notice that the only texts she and Jim had exchanged were from the hospital, waiting for Kenneth to get out of surgery.

I found a treasure trove of vending machines and got us tiny bags of corn chips and pretzels. Do you want anything to drink?

Hoo-yah, thanks, I'd love something with caffeine. :-)

Not exactly romantic.

But Greg wasn't exactly romantic, either, and he'd typed in the text message to Jim that she'd dictated, starting with the bright red flag of *Sweetie*.

Jim was on his way. He had to be, even though he hadn't yet texted her back. But he was smart, he was sharp, he was everything Ashley had ever wanted—except for the flaming asshole part of him.

Still, she knew without a doubt that he *was* on his way.

Bobby and Colleen were still ten minutes out as Jim pulled into Ashley's condo parking lot.

Guest parking was clearly marked, so he pulled into an empty slot even as he quickly looked around, finding the door to her second floor apartment, as well as the stairs that would get him there.

The new password for the surveillance camera app was CJCregg—apparently Ash was a big *West Wing* fan so Bobby had picked something she'd remember—and Jim quickly signed in to get a visual of her living room.

Both she and the gunman were exactly where Bobby had last described them.

Ashley's tiny dining table was in the camera's wide-lens frame, and Jim knew it was no accident that she'd set up her computer there. She sat behind it, frowning as she looked at the screen, while the gunman paced behind her.

He wasn't an operator, that much was clear. Whoever he was, he had little to no firearms training—which potentially made him that much more dangerous in terms of things like accidental discharge.

But something about the way he moved was disconcerting. He was twitchy and sweating. Like he couldn't stay still. Like he was jacked up on cocaine or some type of amphetamine.

Jim zoomed in to look more closely at the room. Ashley's phone was out on a little table near the front door—about fifteen feet away from where she was sitting.

As he impatiently waited for Bobby to arrive, he got out of his truck and quietly closed the door behind him—no need to make Mr. Jumpy jumpier.

It occurred to him that the gunman probably drove there, and one of those other cars parked in that row marked *Guests* probably belonged to the man.

So Jim turned on his phone's flashlight and used it to look inside of each of the vehicles—checking to see if the door was unlocked, or if there was something inside that could help identify who the hell the man was.

Of course, one possible way to take the gunman down was to use his car alarm as a diversion. Set it off in hopes that he'd open the front door to look out to see WTF. But it would help if Jim could figured out which car was his…

It was then that he saw it.

Half covered by a blanket on the backseat of an expensive and shiny new sedan.

An AR-15 assault rifle, with a fucking bump-stock attached.

As Jim looked back at the gunman's twitchy movement and sweaty face in the surveillance feed, he knew with a flash of fear exactly where he'd seen that before. This motherfucker was gonna suicide. Whatever information he was trying to get from Ashley, he was gonna use it to kill as many people as he could before he took his own pathetic life, via suicide-by-SWAT-team.

And he'd probably start his bloody rampage right here, by putting a bullet into Ash's head.

Jim's phone lit with a text—from Colleen. *Still five minutes away.*

He looked at that rifle lying there in that car. Breaking the window to take it *would* set off the car's alarm, only now he did *not* want to do that. No, the only diversion he was willing to risk now was to kick down Ashley's door. It would make the gunman point his weapon at Jim instead of Ashley.

Jim knew he made a big target, but he also knew that a bullet in the gut or chest wouldn't stop him from taking that weapon and ending that motherfucker. Only a headshot could stop a Navy SEAL, and that would require a shit-ton of luck—heads were hard to hit.

But just in case this mofo was unusually lucky, Jim quickly moved his truck to block in the gunman's car, before quietly running for the stairs.

Ashley stalled, sifting through file after file—none of which held the information that Greg was looking for. "It's in here, somewhere, I know it," she told him, "but I have to be honest, Mr. Ramsey, it's highly unlikely the staff at the women's shelter will let you see Betsy at this time of night."

"I'm not worried about that," he told her, and the way he said that made her skin crawl.

"I also want to urge you to call your lawyer," Ashley said. "I feel confident that he can help you."

"He's dead," Greg said, and her heart dropped. "So no, he can't help."

"Okay," she said as now her heart pounded. "Well, then…"

"He didn't have the information I needed," Greg told her.

"Well, I do, I'm sure of it," she said as her brain raced. She'd somehow have to warn the shelter that he was coming. God knows what kind of weapons he had stashed in his car. But God, what if, after she gave him the name of the shelter, he killed her anyway, which would mean she wouldn't be able to warn anyone… "I think I should go with you. To talk to the staff at the shelter—"

Across the room, her phone whooshed with an incoming text. Oh, thank God…

"That's probably Jim," she told Greg. "You should double-check that he's not coming over anyway, to make sure that I'm okay."

Greg crossed the room to where her phone was on the table near the door. "He says, *Tomorrow's great, sweetie. Can't wait to get down and dirty. I love you madly, wish we could do it now.*"

Ashley dropped to the floor.

Get down… do it now…

She had total faith that Jim knew exactly where both she and Greg were, thanks to that security camera.

She heard the door crash open, heard Jim's voice: "Drop the weapon, drop the gun, drop it drop it *drop it*!"

She heard a clatter—no gunshot, thank God—heard a crash that had to be Jim tackling Greg onto her coffee table, shattering it and smashing it flat, and then Jim shouted, "Ash, you okay?"

"I am," she called. "Are you?"

"I'm fine," she heard him say. "Do me a favor and secure this motherfucker's weapon. I kicked it into the kitchen."

She crawled out from beneath her dining room table to see that Jim, indeed, had Greg Ramsey pinned on top of her former coffee table, his arm around Greg's throat, his legs locked around Greg's waist as Greg struggled to get free.

"Define *secure*," she said.

Jim actually laughed. "Start by locating it," he said, in the same almost-gentle, conversational tone he'd used with Kenneth, during the paintball fiasco. "And then, just kinda stand near it. Or, you know, put it in the vegetable drawer in your fridge. Chief Taylor's on his way, FYI, with Skelly and Becker close behind him. Oh, and if you can find your phone after you secure the weapon, it'd probably be good to call 9-1-1."

Her front door was hanging from just one of its hinges. The amount of force Jim had delivered to kick it open... "You need me to get you some ice as long as I'm stashing the gun in the fridge?" she called to him as yes, the gun was right there, on the kitchen floor. She picked it up with her thumb and one finger. Opened the fridge door.

"Nah, I'm... good. Curious, like, who the fuck *is* this since I've already confirmed that he's not Brad."

"His name is Greg Ramsey," she called as she stashed the gun, closed the refrigerator door, and then went looking for her phone. "His wife—ex-wife—is one of my clients. He says he's already killed his lawyer..." And just like that, her matter-of-fact delivery crumbled and her voice broke.

"Ashley, are you okay?" Bobby Taylor was standing just outside her ruined front door. He started to laugh as he took it all in, then came to envelope her in a hug. "I'm guessing Lieutenant Slade decided not to wait."

Jim needed ice—for his shoulder.

He'd hit the floor, hard, when he'd tackled Greg Ramsey.

Kicking in the door was easy enough if you knew how to do it. And yeah, his knees weren't exactly happy with him right now, but they never were.

And it was worth it, entirely, to know that Ashley was safe.

The police had come and taken custody of Ramsey, his refrigerated Glock, and the arsenal in his car. Jim's teammates—Taylor and Skelly and Becker and Lee—had all shown up, ready to assist, and were kind of pissed that he hadn't waited for them.

And yet, they all took one look at the way Jim knew he was looking at Ashley as Colleen kept her arms wrapped tightly around her, and they completely understood.

Waiting had not been an option.

The police finally left, and most of Jim's teammates, too, finally called it a night, and then it was just Bobby Taylor and his wife Colleen, still sitting on the sofa next to Ashley as Jim hovered nearby.

Bobby was ready to board up Ashley's door—using a hammer and nails to secure her condo until the morning, when they could get the door replaced. The plan was for Ash to spend the night at their apartment.

Which was a good idea, but...

"It's late, we should go," Colleen told Ashley. "Do you want to bring your suitcase from Florida, since it's already packed and it's just until tomorrow...?"

It was then that Ashley glanced over at Jim. "Yeah, that's a good idea, but... Will you just give me a minute, to, um..."

"Yes," Colleen said. "Why don't you walk Jim out to his truck. I'll grab your stuff while Bobby boards up the door."

And then, there they were, walking down the steps to the parking lot.

"Thank you," Ashley said. "I knew when I sent that text..."

"*Sweetie*," he said. "I knew right away."

"And when you said that back to me in your text—*Sweetie*—I knew that you knew," she said, laughing a little even though her voice shook. "*Get down and dirty* was inspired."

"*I love you madly*," he said. "That part was real."

But she was shaking her head, stopping as they reached Bobby's car. "Jim, no..."

"Yeah," he said. "And I know that doesn't change anything, I know it's too late, I know I screwed up, but... Ashley, I wish you could at least think about forgiving me. I wish I could explain. I just felt so freaking lost, it was like I was in this giant hole, falling into the darkness, and I had no idea when I was gonna hit the bottom, or how terrible it was gonna be when I splattered, so all I could think was, why would you want me when *I* don't even want me anymore...?"

She started to cry. "You can't tell me that. You're not allowed to say that, and make me feel responsible for—"

"No, please," he said. "Don't feel responsible. That's not why I told you. I'm trying to be honest about what I'm feeling, and I'm not very good at it... But I'm okay. Really. I'm gonna be okay. Everything's gonna be okay. Because nothing could ever be as bad as it was when I was standing out here, thinking this motherfucker was going to kill you. That would've been unbearable. This? All of this is just a road-bump, compared to that. This, I can handle."

But she didn't stop crying. "I'm *so* angry at you. I just can't pretend that you didn't..."

He pulled her into his arms and kissed her, he couldn't not. And she kissed him back—until she pushed him away.

"I can't," she said again. "I'm sorry."

"I know," he whispered. "I just hoped..."

"Thank you for saving my life," she said. "But I can't."

"It's okay," he told her. And because he could see Colleen coming down the stairs, ready to unlock her car to let Ashley in, he walked to his truck, got in, and drove away.

Just like he'd promised Dunk.

CHAPTER SEVENTEEN

Two months later

Luke O'Donlon and his wife Syd were having a baby shower.

Jim had gotten an invite to the party weeks ago, and he'd almost tossed it—the details of where and when, that is. He'd already bought into a group gift being given by SEAL Team Ten—they were rebuilding the side room on the O'Donlon's tiny house, turning it into a combination nursery and playroom.

He was still close to the guys in the team, even though his active duty SEAL days were officially over.

He was doing okay. Mostly.

But as he looked again at that invitation that he'd stuck onto his refrigerator door with a magnet—its cartoon stork and bright letters informing him that the gathering was at the O'Donlon's house on Saturday afternoon—he took out his phone and called Colleen Taylor.

She answered the way she always did—and he'd called her so often over the past few months that they'd become friends. She didn't bother with a greeting. She just—boom—instantly jumped into the conversation. "You coming to the party this weekend?"

"Thinking about it," he said. Colleen had told him a week ago that Ashley was planning to attend. Normally that meant he would stay away. "What do *you* think?"

"What do *I* think?" she asked. "Or what do I think *Ashley* will think, and oh my God, how did I end up back in middle school?"

"I'm trying to be careful," he said. "Respectful. Un-asshole-ish."

"I could send her a note. *Will you hate it if Jim also attends a party given in honor of one of his best friends? Check the box: Yes, I'm heartless and cruel. No, of course not, I expect him to be there.*"

"Mock me, I don't care. Last thing I want is to make her think I'm stalking her, a la Brad."

"Ooh, that reminds me," she said. "Ash *just* had lunch with him, last Wednesday, I think."

"She had lunch," he repeated. "With *Brad*. Like, he called her and said, *Let's have lunch* and she *went…?*"

"I… think he emailed her, but basically, yeah," Colleen said.

"Should I be worried?" he asked. "Damnit, I'm worried."

"Just come to the party," she said. "Sit down next to her, and see what happens. If she stands up and walks away, well, then you'll know."

"Yeah, or maybe she'll bring Brad as her date," Jim said. Jesus, had he waited too long?

"You know that expression, snowball's chance in hell?" Colleen said. "Those are the odds, in my opinion of course, of Ashley getting back with Brad. Just come to the party."

"I don't know anymore," he admitted. "I hurt her really badly. I've been thinking about applying to law school in New York or maybe Boston…"

"With all due respect, Lieutenant, you're a SEAL. I'm married to a SEAL. My brother's a SEAL. I no doubt someday will give birth to a SEAL—and she'll be more kickass than all of you combined. But my point here is that I know SEALs. You walked away from Ashley, because that's what she wanted, but your plan was to walk completely around the world if necessary, so you could *accidentally* meet her again, at some point in the future. This phone call was to ask me if I thought that the future had finally arrived. But only Ashley can answer that. I *can* tell you this: If *I* were a good-looking Navy SEAL rocking a two-months-long beard, who's also spent the last few months borrowing and reading every book on women's issues and intersectional feminism on his teammate's wife's bookshelf—and it's a *big* shelf…? I'd shine myself up, and go celebrate this happy occasion in your good friends' lives, and while you're there, smile at Ashley, and see if she smiles back. If she does, move a little closer—but not too close—and say *Hey, how are you? I miss you.* Then listen to whatever she tells you, and if it's back off, then back off. Why do men find this so hard?"

"I'm a *former* SEAL," he said.

"Oh, my God," Colleen said. "*That's* what you focus on…? Here's a message from my unborn Navy SEAL daughter, Lieutenant: There's no such thing as a *former* SEAL. You make it through BUD/S, you're a SEAL forever, and you know that, so don't be a baby. Come to the party. I'm hanging up now. Man."

Ashley loved spending time with Colleen's friends from SEAL Team Ten, but the baby shower for Lucky and Syd was a slight exception.

This was going to be a *big* party—usually Ashley hung out with Colleen and Bobby, and Colleen's brother Wes and his wife Brittany, and Britt's sister Melody and her husband Harlan, who had the ridiculous nickname, *Cowboy.*

But this time all of Team Ten, past and present, was there—including a high-ranking admiral the women all called *Jake,* but the men all called *Sir.*

Jim Slade was there, too.

He looked... tired. He'd grown a full beard in the months since she'd last seen him, and it was... a very good look for him. His hair was longer, too, but still looked freshly cut. He was wearing a colorful button-down short-sleeved shirt that fit well, hugging his broad shoulders and chest, and showing off both the muscles in his arms and his collection of tattoos. He still wore braces on both knees, but his shorts didn't have multiple cargo pockets—they were khaki and tailored to fit. His transformation, however, didn't quite make it all the way down to his feet. He had on flip-flops, of course, which was the SEAL footwear of choice when boots—or swim-fins—were not an option.

He was in the kitchen when Ashley arrived—he was taking something that smelled delicious out of the oven, but he glanced up and directly into her eyes and smiled, and she flashed both hot and cold as she froze.

"Out of the kitchen!" Wes scolded, going as far as to clap his hands at her. "Men only!"

"We're in charge of food prep," Bobby said.

"And serving, and cleaning up after," Wes's wife Britt added, taking Ashley by the arm and leading her back to the huge deck off the living room, where the party was being held. "As well as all diaper changes and child management. We usually share those duties, but every now and then we impose what we call the Goddess Rule. It's partial payback for when the Team goes wheels up, and the spouses have to do it all. Of course, we're not the ones getting shot at, so there's that..."

Ashley glanced back to see that Jim's tentative smile had faded, and now, as he gazed after her, before turning to the pan of food in his hands, he just looked tired.

But okay. She'd survived that. She hadn't quite managed to say *hello* or even smile back at him, but first steps were good.

"Gifts go there," Britt told her, pointing to a table just inside of the huge sliding glass doors, and Ash added hers to the large pile.

She'd gotten Syd a large stack of her own favorite romance novels, including the latest by Shirley Hailstock, Sarina Bowen, Alyssa Cole, and Alexis Hall. For the last few months of pregnancy, sleep could be elusive, and there was nothing quite as comforting as an old-school printed book.

Britt stepped outside and pointed to a cooler in the shade in the corner. "Beer, soda, wine is over there. Help yourself, and grab a seat."

"Thanks," Ashley said, waving to Colleen—and oh, Dunk was here, too. That was a little awkward, but he smiled and waved, too.

They were sitting beneath an array of colorful umbrellas with most of the other women and at least one other SEAL.

It was gorgeous out there. The big yard's fence was bordered by a jungle of drought-resistant plants, many of which were blooming from the recent rains.

A series of grills were already fired up out in the yard, manned by more SEALs and surrounded by a large, portable play-pen, so the smaller kids couldn't get too close. Ashley could smell both steaks and barbeque—when it came to food, Navy SEALs didn't play around.

On the other side of the yard, Thomas King and Rio Rosetti were refereeing a group of the slightly older kids who were playing croquet. It was then, as Ashley took her wine and sat down in the empty seat next to Colleen, that she realized both of the SEALs sitting in that circle, under the umbrella, were holding babies. Dunk was. As was Dave—a young and relatively new member of Team Ten, who'd gone through BUD/S as one of the first openly gay service-members to be accepted into the program as a SEAL candidate. Not that there hadn't been plenty of gay SEALs before him. But *Don't Ask, Don't Tell* had definitely made life harder for them. It was good that everyone could now live openly and honestly.

"I'm completely in love with her," Dave said now, gazing down at the sleeping baby in his huge arms. He grinned. "Things you generally don't hear me say. Along with *Oh my God, I think maybe I want one.* I mean, not tomorrow, or even next year, but someday…"

Dunk laughed—quietly because the baby he was holding was fast asleep, too. "You might feel differently after spending a little time with a baby who doesn't sleep."

"We had one of those," Commander Catalanotto's wife Veronica chimed in, in her crisp British accent. "We were lucky if we got two uninterrupted hours a night. That child was *hungry.* We threw the rules out the window and started him on rice cereal and he finally slept for four hours straight. That was the night we knew we'd survive."

"Jake took paternity leave because the twins had colic." Zoe had a story, too. "We'd take turns getting up in the night, which only worked in theory, because Jake can sleep through anything. So I'd wake up—when one of the babies cried, I couldn't not hear him—and I'd nudge him and snarl *It's your night,* and he'd stagger into the babies' room. And one night he didn't wake up all the way, but he got out of bed, and I'm lying there going *The baby—I think it's Sam, he's still crying,* and I finally sat up and turned on the light, and I saw that he'd opened the door to the walk-in closet, and he was just standing in there, like, *I know I'm supposed to be doing something, but I'm not sure what…*"

"I will never live that down," Jake came up from his place at the grill and reached over to take and kiss Zoe's hand as the entire group erupted in laughter. "When we celebrate our fiftieth wedding anniversary, Zoe's gonna tell that story."

"You know it," she said, smiling back at him.

A loud clatter from the kitchen made the conversation stop. "Everyone all right in there?" Syd called.

"Guess what, Syd," Luke called back. "Great news! When the party's over, Space and I are gonna clean the interior of the fridge *and* wash the kitchen floor. Hoo-yah!"

"Hoo-yah, indeed!" she called back as she rolled her eyes. "There's a shelf on the door that's broken. It's rigged with duct tape, but it's got a weight limit, and someone always fails to read the memo. This year, apparently, it's Spaceman."

As everyone again laughed, Colleen took the opportunity to lean in and quietly ask, "You okay?"

"Yeah, do I not look okay?" Ashley whispered back.

"You poured yourself a very large glass of wine."

Oh, crap, she had. "I didn't even really want any."

Colleen held out her own plastic "glass," and Ashley gratefully poured half into it, realizing that Col was still whispering to her. "…look great."

Oh, God. "Yeah, he really does, doesn't he?"

"You either didn't or can't hear me," Colleen said. "I said *you* look great."

"Oh," Ashley said. "Thanks. Oh, God. Maybe I should leave. I mean, I had an entire plan figured out, but…"

"Don't you dare," Colleen said.

"So I've been banished from the kitchen," Jim Slade announced.

Ashley looked up to see him coming out onto the deck. His words were aimed at Sydney. "Anything out here you want me to break…?"

There was more laughter, but Colleen stood up since there were no empty chairs. "Here, Space, you can sit here."

Jim looked from her to Ashley. "Oh. Don't I… need to hold a baby to sit out here?"

"I'll go find you one," Colleen said.

"Oh, good," Jim said. "Can you bring me an owner's manual first, because I've never held one and I'm the guy who just broke the freaking refrigerator, so…"

"You've seriously never held a baby?" Brittany asked Jim.

"Don't look at me," Dave said. "I'm not giving up mine. He can find his own baby."

"Mine," Dunk announced, "has just filled his diaper, but even I am not cruel enough to hand him to a newbie like Spaceman Slade. I could use a little assistance, however, both in standing up and getting this monster, I mean sweet angel to the nearest toxic waste removal area, because oh my Jesus God…"

"I got this," Jake said, taking the still sleeping baby from Dunk's arms. "Dear God, you weren't kidding… Come on, Senior. I'll show you how it's done."

"Is it okay if I, um…" Jim was still standing and he pointed to the seat that Colleen had vacated as Ashley realized he was asking her if he could sit.

"Of course," she said. "Yes." As he stepped closer, she realized… "Your toenails are very pink."

"Yes," he said. "They are. Neon, I believe it's called. Joe and Veronica's daughter was offering mani-pedis, and the twins wanted their nails done, but they got into an argument, because some kid at school told one of them that boys couldn't or shouldn't, so I said *Boys, get in line behind me.* And then I said, *Yo, Veronica's Mini-Me, I'll take the neon pink, please. I feel it will work best with both my outfit and skin tone.*"

Ashley laughed as her heart lurched. He was still so... Jim. Which made sense. Just because she'd kept her distance for the past few months didn't mean that he'd stopped being funny and smart. "You were very right."

"Damn straight. I recently watched the new season of *Queer Eye*," he admitted. "I've been spending a lot of time resting my knees."

"That's good."

"Yeah," he said. "I've been studying for the LSATs, and getting ready to apply to law school—my top choice is here in San Diego, of course and... I've also been talking to the team over at JAG. Nobody's made any promises, but we all know I want to stay in the Navy." He smiled wryly. "And not just because I already have the uniforms."

"That's great that you figured that out," Ashley told him, and her heart lurched again as their gazes caught and held and his smile faded.

"Yeah," he said quietly. "I'm getting there, you know. I just keep telling myself progress, not perfection." He cleared his throat. "Hey, how're Kenneth and Clark?"

"Kenneth's great. Completely recovered. Back to eating donuts and drinking beer," she said. "The big twist is that Clark's so completely in love with Kenneth's sister Louise, that *he's* gone gluten-free. She has celiac, remember?"

"Oh, yeah," Jim said. "Wow. Clark still wanna be a SEAL?"

"More than ever," Ashley said. "He's been impressing me a lot lately. I think he might actually do it. I connected him with Kathy Gordon, the chief—my recruiter friend...? After he graduates, I think he's going to join the Navy—as an officer, if you can believe that."

"I can," Jim said. "Absolutely."

"Oh," Ashley said, "*this* is funny. I finally had lunch with Brad. My ex?"

"Oh, I remember Brad. Yes."

"I called him a few days after I got back from camp," Ash said.

"I was done hiding... I called my father, too. I just... pretended I was in command, and I was." She'd told her dad, pretty much pointblank, that she loved him, but she didn't want to live in his cutthroat corporate world. *I know my world is imperfect, but at least here, I have hope for something better...*

"So, how's Brad, um, doing?" Jim asked.

"He's... great," she told him. "He was out of the country when I first called and... anyway, he eventually called me back and he wanted to meet, so I figured why not and... Turns out he's engaged. He's getting married. That's why he showed up, you know, knocking on my door, freaking me out...? He wanted to tell me that, face-to-face."

Jim looked at her. "And... give you a chance to say, *Oh, Brad, please don't...?*"

"Maybe there was a bit of that in there, too," she said. "There *was* a certain stench of creepiness to that lunch, but I was like, *Congratulations!*" She did jazz hands and Jim laughed. "And I *do* hope that he's happy..." She looked at him. "I hope you're happy, too. You seem... well."

Jim nodded. "I'm not sure I'd call it *happy*, but I'm... doing okay. Yeah. You also look... well."

"I am," she said. "Thanks."

But now he was shaking his head. "Yeah, I'm sorry, the word that came out of my mouth was *well*, when what I really meant was *amazing*. You look amazing, and seeing you, and talking to you again is... fucking amazing. I'm sorry if that's too, um, much, or, God, I don't know..."

Ashley interrupted him. "That was also my definition, when I said you looked well. I meant *fucking amazing*, too."

She'd stunned him. Whatever he was expecting her to say, it wasn't that. And now when he met and held her gaze, he was that same man who'd bared his soul to her in Florida. But right now, he couldn't do more than whisper, "Ash...?" It was a question, as if he couldn't quite believe what she'd just said.

So she cleared her throat and clarified. It was, after all, her plan. "I was wondering if you'd maybe want to go out and get... coffee... with me... sometime."

"Oh, thank God!" he said, and for a half a second, she was convinced he was going to cry. But he ran both hands down his face and took a deep breath, and said, "Yes. Please. How about dinner

instead? Tonight? Or you know, drive to Vegas, marry me...?"
She laughed.

"Too soon?"

"Yes," Ashley said. "How about coffee, tomorrow?"

Jim nodded. "Coffee tomorrow works."

"I need to take this slowly," she told him.

"I get it," he said. "I do. What I did was... really shitty. It was inexcusable. And I'm so grateful to have a second chance to show you that... I'm not that guy, that... frightened boy. I'm better than that—or at least I know that I can be. And I... I'm looking forward to letting you have a chance to... get to know me."

Ashley's heart was in her throat. "I really want you... to get to know me, too."

"I would like that very much," he said. "Although I'm pretty sure I knew enough the very first time we talked. I was just too scared and... stupid to know it. I've been working on that, while I was, you know, giving you some space. I'm still working on a lot of things, trying to carve out another option for myself besides manipulative asshole, lying asshole, or idiotic asshole. I think I'm finally getting somewhere with desperate-for-enlightenment-and-desperately-in-love-with-you bonehead."

She laughed her surprise. *Desperately in love...*

But Jim wasn't done. "I'm so freaking imperfect, Ashley," he told her quietly. "But over the past few months, I've learned that I can do this. I can live with the loss of this thing that I love—being a SEAL. Letting it go and moving on. It's still hard, and some days really suck, but... I've been having glimpses of... new purpose and... pride. And I know that I can even... keep going... without you. If I have to. I hope I don't have to. God knows, I don't deserve a second chance, and I'll do my best not to screw it up. But I'm pretty sure I'll make mistakes. More mistakes. I mean, that's kinda how I roll. But here's something I know for sure: my life will be *so* much better with you in it. And I'll work harder than I've ever worked in my life, to learn how to be the partner you deserve."

He sat back in his seat. "And... that was probably too much. Too heavy. I mean, coffee. That's more, *How's Clark*, although we did that. Or maybe, *Hey, what's new with you? I've been trying, but I still can't pull a baseball cap out of my ass.*"

Ashley laughed. And she couldn't resist. It wasn't exactly taking it slowly, but she leaned in and kissed him, and she could taste his surprise. But, as if he knew just how badly and impetuously she was blowing up her own clearly set boundaries, he didn't push it. He didn't pull her in close, or deepen the kiss in any way. He just softly and sweetly kissed her back.

"Oh, thank God," she heard Colleen say.

Ash felt herself blushing as she finally sat back, but then she saw that Jim had tears in his eyes—and he didn't try to hide it. He just looked at her with such hope and yes, *love*.

"Marry me," he whispered.

"Still too soon," she whispered back, but she couldn't hide her smile.

And then Brittany was there, baby in her arms. "This one's mine. His name is Rob—he was named after his favorite uncle, Bobby, and he's five months old. So even *you* probably can't break him, Space, but I'm gonna hang close just in case. You need to support his head—not as much as if he were a newborn, but you can kind of pretend…"

Jim held out his arms and Britt gently nestled her sleepy-eyed son against his chest and he looked down at the baby, who yawned and then smiled as he reached for Jim's nose.

Jim laughed with delight. "He likes me! Holy—"

"No," Britt said flatly.

"Moly," Jim adapted, looking from Britt to Ashley and smiling. "Look at me, capable of learning all kinds of new things."

Ashley smiled. And as she sat back and listened as the SEALs and their spouses gave Jim a lively and laughter-filled crash course in Baby 101, she realized that, for the first time in a long time, she felt grounded. And when Jim turned to her and smiled, when she gazed back into his eyes, she felt as if she'd finally come home.

Coffee, she reminded herself, but she knew that love wasn't possible without taking a risk, without trusting and hoping and sometimes being wrong and getting hurt. And she wanted love, she wanted *home*—she wanted Jim.

But she wanted the real Jim—all of him, not the Jim she thought she'd figured out and knew. And it was going to take a lifetime of learning to truly get to know him.

As Britt finally took Rob back from Jim, as the party rolled on around them, Ashley turned to find him smiling at her. Again.

"So," Ash said. "Everyone here calls you *Space*…?"

Jim laughed. "I seriously haven't told you about my ridiculous nickname…?"

She shook her head.

"Okay. Wow. *Space* is short for *Spaceman*, and I'm going to tell you the real story—the embarrassing one. Cause, you know, the fake story is that I was into NASA as a kid, and I figured I'd enter the space program, become an astronaut by being a SEAL first. Because some guys do that. But that's not why they call me Spaceman."

"It's not?"

"Nope. I had a oxygen tank malfunction during one of my first HAHO jumps. That's when we jump out of an airplane at a high altitude—so high that we need oxygen masks to breathe, or we'll die. My main tank failed and I got hypoxia, which is, you know, lack of oxygen, and it made me hallucinate. And I started talking to Houston and Ground Control because I thought I was in outer space. And the senior chief—it was Randy Duncan, by the way—he's shouting at me to switch to my backup tank. And it wasn't until he, well, he joined me in my little fantasy and he called me *Spaceman Slade*, that I somehow managed to switch tanks. But he couldn't be sure that I'd really done it, because I was, you know, orbiting whatever Class-M planet I thought I was orbiting, so he kept me talking, all the way to the ground. Because hypoxia basically goes hallucination, unconsciousness, death. And if I could talk, I was still conscious. And apparently *Spaceman Slade* had some things to say about boldly going, before the oxygen started working and reality kicked back in."

Ashley had to laugh. "How is that an embarrassing story? You almost died, but you managed to save yourself. With Dunk's help, thank you so much, Dunk."

"Yeah, well, I could've done it more quietly. Saved myself the ridiculous nickname."

"I think, as far as nicknames go, Spaceman's… pretty sexy."

Jim looked at her and didn't say anything although it was very clear that he wanted to. Ashley just waited, and when he finally did speak, he said, "Coffee."

"Coffee," she agreed. "And maybe dinner… next week?"

"I would love that." He nodded. "Okay, Ashley DeWitt. Embarrassing stories. I want to hear 'em all. It's your turn. Go."

Ashley laughed. "I've got *way* too many."

Jim's smile took her breath away. "I've got plenty of time."

Dear Reader,

SEAL Camp is the twelfth book in my *Tall, Dark & Dangerous* series about Navy SEAL Team Ten. Like all TDD installments, even though *SEAL Camp* features characters who have appeared earlier in the series, the book stands alone. (Navy SEAL Lieutenant Jim "Spaceman" Slade and Colleen Skelly Taylor's former roommate, Ashley DeWitt, both appeared in *Taylor's Temptation* (TDD #10), but didn't manage to meet until now!)

But... because *Night Watch*, the last book in my TDD series, was published way back in 2003 (a variety of issues made me put the series on hold), when I finally wrote *SEAL Camp*, I was faced with a choice. Should I maintain the old timeline and set this book in the early 2000s...? (Pagers! Dial-up internet! Ugh! No!!) Or... should I maintain the old timeline, acknowledge the passage of time, and set the story in the current day...? (By which point even the youngest SEALs in the series would probably be retired, so all of the familiar faces would be gone. Ugh! No!!)

Or...

Should I do one of those funky, weird, kinda cheat-y, soap-opera-esque thangs, and warp time so that we (me-the-writer and you-the-reader) could have it all...? (Smart phones! Text messages! Wi-fi! *And* familiar names and faces! Yes!!)

So yeah. As I mentioned in that little note right at the top of Chapter One, *SEAL Camp* is set *both* in the present day, *and* about a year and a half after the end of *Night Watch* (TDD #11, Wes and Brittany's book). Team CO Captain Joe Catalanotto, and Senior Chief Harvard Becker, and Lieutenant Jim Slade, and Lucky and Bobby and Wes and most of the rest of the SEALs have been in their early-to-mid-to-late-thirties for more than a dozen years. (Gee, I wish I could say the same!) Thomas King and Rio Rosetti and Mike Lee are still the young "tadpoles" of the Team. Although there's even a newer new-guy, a SEAL named Dave. (Yeah, you'll be seeing more of Dave.)

And for those readers out there who have helped make "Will you ever write Thomas and Tasha's story?" my all-time *most* frequently asked FAQ, my answer is an all-caps *YES*. In case you didn't notice, LT (jg) Thomas King is on deck as a hero. He may not be next (I've got my eye on Dunk, too…) but it's definitely time to write his book.

If you enjoyed *SEAL Camp*, I'd appreciate it greatly if you'd post a review or toss it some shiny stars and/or digital buckets o' love at your favorite on-line bookseller. You might've noticed that I've become an indie author, and I'm my own publisher now. (Ah, the freedom! OMG, the typos are now all mine!)

But authors, particularly indie authors, depend on reader reviews more than ever in this crazy, noisy, option-filled digital world. I'm very grateful, too, when you post, share, tweet, text, and talk about my books, particularly new ones like *SEAL Camp*! (Thank you so very, very much!)

I'm also producing—and writing—movies these days, with a focus on LGBTQ rom-coms. I *just* finished writing a screenplay for a romantic comedy called *Out of Body* that we're going to be filming in summer 2018. (Watch for our Kickstarter!! How? Sign up for my e-newsletter!!)

And be sure to check out *Analysis Paralysis*, a rom-com movie that I produced—written and directed by and starring my amazing son, Jason T. Gaffney. (It's funny AF. I've watched it 2,748 times in post, and I *still* laugh!!)

Last but way not least, thank you for choosing to spend your precious reading time with my characters and me. Life is crazy these days (Spring 2018), with daily stressors that are enormous! (Please register and #VoteBlue!)

I love getting interactive: Twitter's my social media format of choice—give me a shout @SuzBrockmann. And if you want to be absolutely certain you'll get hot-off-the-press news about upcoming new releases (like that TDD book about Thomas and Tasha!), reissues, appearances, and e-book deals, sign up for my e-newsletter at https://tinyletter.com/SuzanneBrockmann !!

Love and hugs and don't stop fighting for equality, hope, peace, and love,

Suzanne Brockmann

More from Suzanne Brockmann:

Troubleshooters Series
1. *The Unsung Hero*
2. *The Defiant Hero*
3. *Over the Edge*
4. *Out of Control*
5. *Into the Night*
6. *Gone Too Far*
7. *Flashpoint*
8. *Hot Target*
9. *Breaking Point*
10. *Into the Storm*
11. *Force of Nature*
12. *All Through the Night*
13. *Into the Fire*
14. *Dark of Night*
15. *Hot Pursuit*
16. *Breaking the Rules*
17. *Headed for Trouble* (anthology)
18. *Do or Die*
19. *Some Kind of Hero*

Troubleshooters Short Stories and Novellas
1. *When Tony Met Adam*
2. *Beginnings and Ends*
   (A Jules & Robin Short Story)
3. *Free Fall*
4. *Home Fire Inferno*
5. *Ready to Roll*
6. *Murphy's Law*

Tall, Dark & Dangerous Series
1. *Prince Joe*
2. *Forever Blue*
3. *Frisco's Kid*
4. *Everyday, Average Jones*
5. *Harvard's Education*
6. *Hawken's Heart*
   (It Came Upon a Midnight Clear)
7. *The Admiral's Bride*
8. *Identity: Unknown*
9. *Get Lucky*
10. *Taylor's Temptation*
11. *Night Watch (Wild, Wild Wes)*
12. *SEAL Camp*

Fighting Destiny Paranormal Series
0.5 *Shane's Last Stand (e-short prequel)*
1. *Born to Darkness*

Night Sky YA Series
(with Melanie Brockmann)
0.5 *Dangerous Destiny*
   (e-short prequel)
1. *Night Sky*
2. *Wild Sky*

Stand-Alone Romance
HeartThrob
Body Language
Embraced by Love
Future Perfect
Give Me Liberty
Ladies' Man
Stand-in Groom
Letters to Kelly
Scenes of Passion
Undercover Princess
(Rita Award Winner)

Sunrise Key Series
1. *Kiss and Tell*
2. *The Kissing Game*
3. *Otherwise Engaged*

Stand-Alone Romantic Suspense
Body Guard (Rita Award winner)
Infamous
Time Enough For Love
Hero Under Cover
Love With the Proper Stranger
No Ordinary Man

Bartlett Brothers Series
1. *Forbidden*
2. *Freedom's Price*

St. Simone Series
1. *Not Without Risk*
2. *A Man to Die For*

ABOUT THE AUTHOR

After childhood plans to become the captain of a starship didn't pan out, **Suzanne Brockmann** took her fascination with military history, her respect for the men and women who serve, her reverence for diversity, and her love of storytelling, and explored brave new worlds as a *New York Times* bestselling romance author. Over the past twenty-five years she has written fifty-seven novels, including her award-winning Troubleshooters series about Navy SEAL heroes and the women—and sometimes men—who win their hearts. In addition to writing books, Suzanne Brockmann produces feature-length movies: the award-winning romantic comedy *The Perfect Wedding*, which she co-wrote with her husband, Ed Gaffney, and their son, Jason; the thriller *Russian Doll*; and the soon-to-be-released rom-com *Analysis Paralysis*. She is currently in pre-production for *Out of Body*, a rom-com with paranormal elements. She has also co-written two YA novels with her daughter Melanie, and is the publisher and editor of an m/m line of category romances called *Suzanne Brockmann Presents*. Her latest novel is *SEAL Camp*, available in print and e-book from Suzanne Brockmann Books.

Website: www.SuzanneBrockmann.com
e-Newsletter: www.tinyletter.com/SuzanneBrockmann
Twitter: @SuzBrockmann
Facebook: www.Facebook.com/SuzanneBrockmannBooks